Bolan shifted his aim to the three gunmen who were directing fire his way

Holding the submachine gun at waist level, he sprang from behind the cover of the tree and dashed forward, angling his way toward an outcropping of rocks. While he ran, he fired the Spectre in short bursts, engaging targets of opportunity as they appeared.

Bullets were flying through the air as Bolan launched himself into a dive that would take him to his intended spot behind the rocks. He felt the sudden sting of a round scratch the top of his scalp. He twisted in midair to direct his reply at the shooter, sending a burst of a dozen slugs into him and the man who knelt nearby.

"How're you doing?" he asked into the mike as he grabbed one of his two remaining box magazines to replace the spent one.

"The M-60 is out," LaFontaine shouted back.

"Throw the smoke and give me cover. I have plastique for the four corners. Let's blow this building!" the Executioner shouted.

MACK BOLAN ®
The Executioner

The Executioner®
Don Pendleton's

BLACK DEATH REPRISE

A GOLD EAGLE BOOK FROM

WORLDWIDE®

TORONTO • NEW YORK • LONDON
AMSTERDAM • PARIS • SYDNEY • HAMBURG
STOCKHOLM • ATHENS • TOKYO • MILAN
MADRID • WARSAW • BUDAPEST • AUCKLAND

. First edition April 2008

ISBN-13: 978-0-373-64353-0
ISBN-10:   0-373-64353-5

Special thanks and acknowledgment to
Peter Spring for his contribution to this work.

BLACK DEATH REPRISE

To lead an untrained people to war is to throw them away.

—Confucius, 551–479 BC

Evil men lead blind followers into battle unprepared for what they will face. What they will face is me—their Executioner.

—Mack Bolan

THE
MACK BOLAN

LEGEND

Nothing less than a war could have fashioned the destiny of the man called Mack Bolan. Bolan earned the Executioner title in the jungle hell of Vietnam.

But this soldier also wore another name—Sergeant Mercy. He was so tagged because of the compassion he showed to wounded comrades-in-arms and Vietnamese civilians.

Mack Bolan's second tour of duty ended prematurely when he was given emergency leave to return home and bury his family, victims of the Mob. Then he declared a one-man war against the Mafia.

He confronted the Families head-on from coast to coast, and soon a hope of victory began to appear. But Bolan had broken society's every rule. That same society started gunning for this elusive warrior—to no avail.

So Bolan was offered amnesty to work within the system against terrorism. This time, as an employee of Uncle Sam, Bolan became Colonel John Phoenix. With a command center at Stony Man Farm in Virginia, he and his new allies—Able Team and Phoenix Force—waged relentless war on a new adversary: the KGB.

But when his one true love, April Rose, died at the hands of the Soviet terror machine, Bolan severed all ties with Establishment authority.

Now, after a lengthy lone-wolf struggle and much soul-searching, the Executioner has agreed to enter an "arm's-length" alliance with his government once more, reserving the right to pursue personal missions in his Everlasting War.

A gentle breeze passing through the vineyard from the Pyrenees turned the leaves on their stems, making them appear to be waving to the man who glided silently through their tethered rows. The soothing rustle as they stirred on warm air currents, exposing undersides that shimmered a silvery-gray in the moonlight, was the only sound reaching Mack Bolan's ears as he trod silently across the fertile fields that for more than eight hundred years had been producing wine for the St. Rafael Monastery north of Bayonne.

Dressed entirely in black, with green and brown camouflage paint smeared on the high points of his face to flatten his features, Bolan's large frame was all but invisible against the inky French countryside.

On his hip, the ex-soldier wore a .44 Magnum Desert Eagle, while a holster on his left shoulder held a Beretta 93-R loaded with a 20-round clip of 9 mm Parabellum ammunition. A foot-long Fairbairn-Sykes combat knife, honed to a razor's edge, rested in a weathered black leather sheath strapped to the outside of his right calf.

Bolan was approaching the monastery from the south because slipping into Spain at San Sebastian and traveling by car through the Pyrenees mountains to Bayonne was considerably easier for a heavily armed man than trying to fly into an airport, whether public or private, anywhere in France. The one hundred rounds of ammunition he brought for the Desert Eagle would have been impossible to get through French customs—never mind the concussion grenades and incendiary tape he carried in the pouches on his combat web belt.

As would most battle-tested veterans with whom death has become intimate enough to be a frequent visitor to their dreams, the man some called the Executioner was hoping not to use his weapons this night. But he had been schooled on the hellfire trail in distant jungles long enough to know firsthand that hope and death were frequent bedfellows. Those who came unprepared to kill at a moment's notice, surrendering their fate to optimism or hope, were the ones who found themselves easy targets when a supposedly cold spot turned unexpectedly hot.

Despite the vineyard's tranquil appearance, two CIA agents had been murdered there less than a week earlier, the homing device implanted in one's deltoid muscle leading the Agency to a wooded area ten miles north, where the operatives' bullet-ridden bodies had been discovered in a shallow grave. They had met their deaths while on the mission now assigned to Bolan—to rescue Dr. Zagorski from the confines of the ancient abbey.

Bolan's Porsche 911 Turbo was hidden in a stand of trees about a mile south of the monastery where he had left it in order to approach his objective on foot, a tactic yielding the greatest variety of options. When combat veterans gained enough experience under fire, they learned that flexibility on the battlefield was what survival was all about—the soldier who ran out of options first was the one who died.

The choppy sound of helicopter blades cutting the air shattered the vineyard's stillness with a noise that touched nerve endings buried deep within Bolan's warrior psyche. He lowered himself to the ground, pressing his body against the single strand of heavy zinc wire. It ran about six inches above the soil the entire length of each row, alternately weaving inside and outside the slender trunks of adjacent vines, connecting an entire row into a supporting network able to withstand the rainstorms that rushed down the rugged slopes of the Pyrenees. The tended vines were leafless for the bottom two feet or so, forming a canopy under which Bolan would be concealed from the passing aircraft. Lying on his back, motionless to prevent an errant move from catching the eye of an alert passenger in the chopper, he waited for it to pass.

Coming straight across the vineyard, the helicopter was apparently not searching for intruders. As it whizzed past on a direct course for the monastery, more than ten rows to the right of where Bolan lay as still as a statue, he was able to see it was the Bell 206B-3 JetRanger that Hal Brognola told him the Order of Raphael had purchased six months earlier to replace their aging Hughes 300C. The new helicopter carried two-and-a-half times more weight, had room for four passengers and was almost twice as fast as the Hughes.

Bolan remained in place as he watched the chopper reach its destination. Abruptly illuminated by the landing pad's powerful lights, it hovered like an apparition for a few moments before descending slowly out of sight. From satellite reconnaissance photos he had studied back at Stony Man Farm, Bolan knew the landing pad was a mere thirty yards from a guarded entrance to the research laboratory that was his objective.

The helicopter's engine tapered off into silence, the landing pad's lights were turned off, and once again, a hush as deep as prayer blanketed the vineyard.

Bolan rose, touch-checking his gear before resuming. As he set off toward the base of the hill on top of which the ancient L'Abbaye de Raphael sat, he recalled the conversation with Hal Brognola two days earlier that had brought him to the South of France for his mission.

"THE CONSEQUENCES ARE too horrific for the President to ignore," Brognola had said at their meeting on the National Mall in Washington.

The man from the Justice Department was fully aware of the arm's-length relationship Bolan held with the federal government even when his sense of righteousness was inflamed to the point where he accepted a mission, so he wasn't about to beg or plead. Bolan would decide on his own whether to sign on, and that would be that.

Brognola swallowed hard, said, "This is much more than a random terrorist group developing something like anthrax, or getting their hands on a batch of nerve agent. At least we can contain those threats. A project like this could jeopardize humankind's very existence."

He paused for a moment before adding, "Jesus, Striker, the plague was devastating the first time around. No one wants to see an updated version."

They were walking west along the Mall's boundary on Madison Drive, the brilliantly white Capitol Building shimmering at their backs under the unrelenting sun. As he walked, Brognola mopped his face with one of the cotton handkerchiefs he carried during Washington summers.

Outside the Smithsonian Castle, Bolan could see a group

of tourists, mostly families with kids out of school for the summer, clustered around an idling tour bus. Their limp hair and sagging postures told him long before he came into earshot of the children's whining voices that they had been outdoors in the brutal humidity for a while.

Bolan himself showed no sign of the heat. He was dressed in pressed khaki pants and a navy blue golf shirt. The portion of his face visible under his dark glasses gleamed in the sunlight with a vibrant glow akin to that produced by the light film of oil that coated the ex-soldier's handguns.

"Terrorists won't fly airplanes into buildings anymore," Brognola said as Bolan studied the transcript from the Oval Office while they walked. "They'll escalate their tactics by using science and state-of-the-art technology to develop more exotic weapons of mass destruction. The news is full of the bird flu. What we're talking about here has the potential to be ten, maybe a hundred, times more dangerous. A designer disease with its genetic roots reaching all the way back to the Black Death? Tell me that's not a doomsday scenario."

"How sure are they?" Bolan asked. "The government's track record for getting good intel is an embarrassment."

At the junction of Madison with Twelfth Street, a dozen college-aged girls were sunbathing on the heavy concrete slabs outside the National Museum of American History. As Bolan walked past the building's front lawn, he could smell the pineapple and coconut fragrances from their tanning lotions.

"This time the CIA has French verification," Brognola answered. "INSERM doctors working with Sentinelles have forensic evidence from animal carcasses. Someone is definitely mucking around with genetically engineered diseases."

"And why do they think the carcasses came from—" Bolan hesitated until a group of schoolchildren heading toward the Capitol passed them "—the Order of Raphael?"

They had reached the Washington Monument, the 555-foot marble obelisk pointing ramrod straight into the sky. Brognola steered them to the right, onto Constitution Avenue, waiting until they had distanced themselves a few yards from the closest tourist before saying, "The Order is centuries old, dating all the way back to before the Crusades. Today, they're a fully modern paramilitary organization with a few hundred members in France, the United States and Australia. Their American office is in Boston. Almost a year ago, they caught Homeland Security's attention. They—"

Bolan interrupted by asking, "What triggered the initial alert?"

"Cell phone patterns. The NSA's eavesdropping programs recognized words spoken during the Order's calls to and from Boston and the monastery at Bayonne. That led directly to Internet surveillance and an on-site CIA probe. The more we pulled the string, the more the Order of Raphael looked like a terrorist organization."

"But the CIA didn't find anything in Boston or France?" Bolan asked.

"No. There's a lab at Bayonne—no law against independent research—and the Agency mined the databases of medical supply houses and uncovered sales documents relating to scientific equipment and supplies. But when Dr. Zagorski was kidnapped from her home outside Paris three months ago, the French authorities suddenly became as interested in the Order as we were."

"Hold on," Bolan said while flipping through the five-page report to find and reread the section mentioning the scientist. "Okay. What's her story?"

At the far west end of the park, Brognola could see the sloping walls of the Vietnam Veterans' Memorial, crowded as always with loved ones seeking healing from a generation-old wound.

Brognola kept his eyes on the monument in the distance as he answered Bolan's question. "Sonia Zagorski is one of the world's leading virologists. Shortly after her disappearance, L'Abbaye de Raphael ordered some very specific equipment. Right down to model numbers, it was the same stuff Dr. Zagorski had in her Paris lab."

"If the French and the CIA both believed that Zagorski had been kidnapped by the Order of Raphael, why didn't they raid the place?" Bolan asked.

"Interpol did. Two months ago. They didn't find any trace of her or the new equipment we know the Order bought. Since then, our satellite flyovers have recorded increased security around the monastery with roving guards and limited access to outside suppliers like the electric company and water providers. Homeland Security says the Order is definitely lowering its profile, but we're still monitoring a ton of coded phone calls, encrypted Internet traffic and scientific purchases. Agents McCabe and Gardner were sent in the night before last for what should have been a soft probe. Langley thinks they were ambushed—neither of their weapons had been fired."

Bolan continued reading the report, his mouth drawn into a thin line as he turned back to review an earlier portion.

Brognola said, "With the war in Iraq, we aren't on the best of terms with France right now. The President wants someone independent to get in there and rescue Zagorski."

Independent, Bolan thought. How many times had he accepted missions knowing that if he was caught, his government would deny knowing him? Granted it was the path he had chosen when life had nothing left to offer, but sometimes he questioned his very existence. He knew he'd eventually find himself in a hot zone out of control, and that's where it would all end. Was hoping that he went out honorably, a warrior in the heat of battle, the best his future could offer?

"If she doesn't want to be rescued, I won't know until it's too late. Too late for her to be anything more than an obstacle blocking my escape," Bolan stated.

Brognola looked away, wiping his handkerchief across his brow. "Nothing indicates she's connected to the Order in any way," he said.

"Okay," Bolan said abruptly, handing the file back to Brognola.

They parted without another word, the man from Justice setting off to inform the President that his request had been accepted. Bolan quickly melted into the swells of Washington tourists the way a tiger melted into the jungle.

AT THE EDGE OF A VINEYARD four thousand miles from the spot where he had first learned of a place called L'Abbaye de Raphael, Mack Bolan dropped to one knee and reached into the pouch on his web belt containing his night-vision goggles.

Manufactured by American Technologies Network Corporation, the Gen IV vision system employed XR-5 technology and infrared illumination, which meant the ultra-lightweight gallium arsenide tubes could render a completely dark night into an eerie green landscape as bright as noontime. With the moon peeking every now and then from behind sporadic clouds in a sky filled with stars, night vision was not Bolan's primary need.

He switched the goggles into infrared mode, and the scene before him shimmered slightly for a few moments while the photocathode sensors adjusted to the new data stream. At the base of the hill, laser-crisp infrared beams became visible, crisscrossing the approach to stone steps leading up to the monastery. To the left, a two-lane road wound up and around the side of the hill.

Bolan scanned the landscape before him, searching for additional infrared security nets. Agents McCabe and Gardner, he thought, had to have broken one of the beams, announcing their presence without even knowing it. There were three other hot spots at various points on the hill, but none in the vicinity of the road.

As Bolan removed his goggles, he recalled the reconnaissance photos he had studied at Stony Man Farm. The lab's entrance was shielded from the road by a thin stand of trees running almost to the top, which meant he could approach on the asphalt until he got close.

His gaze moved to the field's northwest corner, where six all-terrain vehicles hitched to open carts containing gardening tools were parked in a straight line pointing south into the vineyard. When he reached the first, Bolan stopped to inspect its controls. Using his foot-long combat knife to pry open the instrument panel, he bent close to examine the three-wheeler's ignition wiring. A bird cried out in the distance, and the warrior paused while listening hard. Crickets close by chirped a summer symphony in tune with their reproductive cycles. From all other directions, the buzzing and humming of night insects reaching his ears reassured him that he was the only human in the immediate vicinity.

Over the years, on battlefields spanning the globe, Bolan had hot-wired vehicles ranging from dune buggies to M-60 tanks. ATVs were at the low end of the technology continuum. Even in the dark, it took him less than a minute to cut, strip and splice the on-off toggle switch into a hot connection bypassing the ignition key. After dipping his finger into the fuel tank to check the vehicle's gas level, he unhooked the tool cart from the ATV, pushing it a few feet to the rear.

As he passed each of the remaining five on his way to the access road, he paused for a moment to pierce their wide front tires with his scalpel-sharp combat knife, rendering all but the one he had hot-wired inoperable. Bolan didn't know if he'd need an ATV on his way out, but disabling all except one created an option.

With a final glance over his shoulder, he stepped onto the asphalt, leaning slightly into the incline.

The road's rise was steep, curling like a corkscrew up the side of the hill to a plateau on which the ancient L'Abbaye de Raphael stood. Shortly before the road leveled out, Bolan entered the sparse woods surrounding the compound. Moving through the underbrush as silently as a shadow, he reached a concealed spot thirty yards from the helipad.

In accordance with its construction period, the stone monastery was built like a medieval fortress, occupying an area roughly half that of a city block. Rounded parapets protected each corner from assault, and it wasn't hard to imagine defenders on top of the turrets dumping scalding liquids onto invaders attempting to scale the walls. Bolan already knew there were no windows on the first floor, leaving the front and rear porticos, with buttressed stone archways too narrow to accommodate greater than three men abreast, as the only means of entry from ground level.

Two guards armed with Fabrique Nationale Herstal P-90 submachine guns stood at the entrance beyond the helipad, their presence negating any possibility of unauthorized access. Bolan hadn't expected to waltz through the laboratory's front door, but he wanted to view it nevertheless. He took the opportunity to examine his opponents' hardware.

In addition to their submachine guns, the sentries wore shoulder holsters carrying FN Five-seveNs. Weighing a mere 1.6 pounds, the Belgium-made pistol used the same 5.7 mm ammunition as the P-90, fed from a clip holding twenty rounds. Although the lightweight handguns lacked the punch that a 9 mm Glock or a Smith & Wesson .45 might deliver, its bullets were available in a version with steel-hardened tips that penetrated Kevlar, making them the ideal choice when anticipating an assault by law-enforcement personnel.

Pulling his goggles over his eyes in order to see the pockets of infrared security placed randomly around the monastery's perimeter, Bolan inched away from the helipad. The natural foliage was plenty thick to provide good concealment, but it was also short, forcing him to circle the building by alternating between a low crawl and half-crouched sprints until he came to the side he had selected ahead of time from the satellite photos.

In person, the side wall was exactly what he expected. It was close enough to the woods to enable a swift approach, and angled in a way that placed it out of sight from the driveways leading to the front and rear entrances. Most importantly, a window approximately sixty feet off the ground, which Bolan believed was the lab's only escape route, gleamed brightly against the cold stone walls under the enhanced ambient moonlight created by the goggles. Dropping to one knee, he scanned the wall and area directly beneath, ensuring there were no infrared sensors.

From one of the pouches on his web belt, he withdrew a folding titanium grappling hook tied to a coiled length of thin cord resembling braided dental floss. Developed at NASA by the same team responsible for giving the world Velcro, a three-hundred-foot length was fine enough to fold entirely into the palm of his hand while possessing all the strength of mountaineering rope.

After locking the grappling tines into their open position so they formed a claw resembling an eagle's talons, Bolan stepped from the woods. While walking toward the building, he began swinging the hook in an increasing arc above his head, playing out the line until he felt the proper tug. When the twine started vibrating slightly in response to the pull exerted by the hook's momentum, he twirled and snapped his wrist with the finesse of an accomplished fly fisherman, releasing the grappling hook onto a trajectory that sent it sailing over the two-hundred-foot-high wall more than thirty feet to the left of the lab window. Using a hand-over-hand motion to pull in the slack, he found that the hook had caught purchase on his first try.

Before scaling the building, Bolan pushed the goggles onto his forehead where he'd be able to pull them quickly into place if needed. He checked his watch. Two patrolling guards were due to make their rounds within ten minutes, but if they stayed true to the schedule Homeland Security had recorded throughout the previous three weeks of satellite flyovers, Bolan had plenty of time to make his ascent.

Drawing the Beretta from his shoulder holster, he checked the sound suppressor while making sure the safety was off. With one hand, he placed the pistol under the strap holding his knife sheath in place on his outer calf where it would be readily accessible. With the other, he grabbed the thin cord and pulled with all his weight. The line remained taut, and after taking a moment to secure the rest of his gear, he began walking up the side of the fortress like a human fly.

The wall was rough, with thick mortar seams and uneven joints making it easy to climb. As Bolan moved higher, he looped the line around his left hand and elbow, taking in the slack his ascent created.

The assault occurred at approximately seventy feet above ground, when a colony of between ten and fifteen short-nosed fruit bats, apparently attracted by the supersonic whine emanating from Bolan's infrared goggles, attacked as if they were a school of airborne piranha. With a frantic fluttering of papery wings accompanied by barely audible squeaks, the furry mammals zeroed in on the soldier's face and neck, biting and scratching with tiny claws as they sought the source of the offending noise.

Wrapping the scaling cord tightly around his left hand in order to free his right, Bolan planted his feet onto the wall and leaned away until he was parallel to the ground. The extended position shifted his entire weight onto his left forearm, causing the tendons to stand out like steel cables stretched to the point of snapping. While reaching up with his freed right hand to switch the goggles' power switch to the off position, he swatted the bats away from his face and head. Once the goggles were turned off, the colony departed as abruptly as they had arrived, leaving Bolan hanging straight out at a right angle from the rock wall.

An image flashed through his mind of a previous mission conducted years earlier in the tropical jungles of Guatemala when his five-man task force had been attacked by a similar colony of short-nosed bats. Assuming that most wild bats were rabid, the men who had been bitten were afraid they were destined to die a horrible death until one of them who had studied the animals ensured the group that the species' reputation was undeserved.

Bolan knew bats had a relatively low probability of carrying rabies, much less than for other mammals such as raccoons or skunks. And when the disease did strike, it would wipe out an entire colony within weeks, limiting the communicable danger to a very narrow time period.

As he pulled on the scaling cord to bring himself into a more upright posture, Bolan knew that the guards he suddenly heard coming around the corner of the north parapet posed a much greater threat to his life than the bites and scratches that stung his face and neck in a dozen places.

Upon hearing the sentries, Bolan immediately stopped reeling himself into the wall, halting when he was still at a forty-five-degree angle to the rough surface. Moving in ultra-slow motion, he drew his Beretta 93-R from the strap holding his knife sheath in place and waited for the men below to pass by.

Since he was unable to use his goggles, Bolan couldn't get a good look at the guards, but from the sounds reaching his ears, he thought they were walking with rifles slung behind their shoulders. The play in the metal clasp where a sling attached to a weapon's stock created a distinctive click he had heard thousands of times coming from soldiers with their weapons carried at sling arms.

As they approached his position, he tracked them with his

93-R, hoping they would pass without incident. Not that the combat veteran was adverse to killing them both if they so much as looked up—countless corpses littering hellfire trails across the globe were testament to his willingness to survive at all costs—but Bolan found no pleasure in taking life. He was a quintessential soldier, willing to answer the call of duty as defined by his personal values, but he would not kill cavalierly. Despite a career testifying to the contrary, he held a deep respect for the sanctity of life.

The guards were progressing at a steady pace that would bring them directly below his spot in less than a minute. They were speaking softly in French, their tone and cadence causing Bolan to think they were reciting scripture. Beneath his feet, he could suddenly feel a section of the ancient mortar begin to shift under the burden of his angled weight, sending tiny pieces of centuries-old limestone trickling noisily down the wall.

The men looked up, and appearing as if they were performing a synchronized move they had rehearsed a thousand times, grabbed to pull the rifles off their shoulders.

Bolan's Beretta coughed twice within the span of a second.

The first round caught a guard square in his upturned face, delivering 9 mm Parabellum lead that jerked his head back while lifting him entirely off his feet. He landed two or three yards away, dead before his body impacted the ground.

His partner was hit in the neck, the force of the steel-jacketed slug spinning him in a graceful pirouette while his severed carotid artery sprayed a crimson geyser, making him resemble for a few moments a pulsating lawn sprinkler. As he crumpled to the ground, his heart pumped four or five progressively smaller spurts, which, under the moonlight, took on a rich black hue.

Bolan slid swiftly down the line, intent on hiding the bodies. He knew his entry would eventually be discovered and he'd be forced to fight his way out, but the longer his presence and his point of access remained unknown, the better his chances for getting away with Dr. Zagorski. When he reached the ground, he dragged the corpses into the woods where he arranged them out of sight behind a clump of elms.

A passing cloud cleared the face of the moon, and in the improved light, an oddity caught Bolan's eye. Both guards possessed what appeared to be identical diamond-shaped scars about the size of a dime on the back of their left hands, the rough tissue standing out in the silvery moonlight against the smoother neighboring skin. As he turned away from the bodies to resume his entry, the soldier filed the detail into a corner of his mind.

Without the encumbrance of the bats, Bolan's second attempt to scale the wall went quickly. There was no barrier at the top, and he easily pulled himself over the turret's lip with one arm. Although none of the satellite photos he had studied contained evidence of a roof patrol, Bolan held his Beretta 93-R in his free hand as he came over the parapet, landing softly on the roof's pebbly surface. When he was sure he was alone, he retrieved the grappling hook and pushed it into its pouch, laying the bunched cord on top.

Occupying the same footprint as the building it capped, the roof's area was large. Air pumps and condensers for heating systems were arranged in groups interspaced among communication antennas across the top of the ancient building, indicating various heating and communication zones within. Moving in a crouch to reduce his silhouette, Bolan walked straight to the northwest corner, where a series of unique vents and ductwork characteristic of research laboratories sprouted in the shadow of huge air conditioning units like wild orchards on the floor of a redwood forest. Although the air intake tunnel was large enough for a man to enter, a heavy metal grate had been spot-welded across the opening.

From a pouch on his web belt next to where he carried two M-18 smoke canisters, Bolan withdrew a roll of incendiary tape and a small plastic tube containing a substance like petroleum jelly. Using his combat knife, he cut short sections from the half-inch roll and wound them around each of the dozen crossbeams where the grate was welded to the tunnel's frame. The tape's active ingredient was a waxy allotrope of white phosphorous that CIA scientists had altered to prevent its reaction to atmospheric oxygen, thus making it a portable product. They had also developed a reagent designed to eliminate the dense white smoke white phosphorous usually produced while burning, which in addition to being undesirably visible, also contained toxic amounts of both phosphorous pentoxide and phosphoric acid.

Once the tape was in place, Bolan used his combat knife to slice open one end of the tube and quickly smear a dollop of the reagent onto each piece. The goop was a sodium-based oxidant that would react in about a minute with the white phosphorous in the tape, bringing it to its flash point.

Once the tape was coated, Bolan averted his eyes and stood close to the grate in an attempt to shield the flashes. The tape buzzed briefly before bursting into a white-hot exothermic flame, each section of tape igniting in the order

Bolan had applied the reactant. The burn-through was quick, less than five seconds, but it had taken slightly longer than fifteen to touch every section, which meant the light intensity peaked at seven seconds for a three-second period before dimming. When the tape wrapping the final crossbeam winked out, Bolan dropped to one knee, drawing his handguns. After remaining motionless for slightly longer than a minute, he concluded that the light from the burning white phosphorous had not been seen.

Holstering both his Desert Eagle and Beretta, he grasped the grate in the middle of its grid and pulled it away from the air vent. Before he climbed into the metal tunnel, he adjusted the night goggles over his eyes and switched the unit into IR mode. Seeing no infrared beams blocking his way, he moved headfirst into the vent.

As he progressed through the air tunnel, Bolan recalled the schematic Akira Tokaido had created on the bank of Cray SV2 supercomputers housed at Stony Man Farm. Using sonar data downloaded from satellite flyovers, the talented hacker had been able to produce a three-dimensional map charting air tunnels from the roof leading into the research lab.

"IT'S KIND OF LIKE AN echocardiogram," Akira Tokaido had told Bolan while nodding slightly to the rhythm of rock music blasting through his ever present earbuds, "just not as accurate."

"But you're sure these vents lead into the lab?"

"Not exactly, Striker," Aaron "The Bear" Kurtzman, head of the cybernetics team at Stony Man Farm had answered for his subordinate. "We have good photos of the roof. There's no question these are not general air conditioning or heating inlets. We're assuming they must be laboratory exhaust and intake. For the type of research Dr. Zagorski does, you'd want a dedicated air system. These fit the bill. We believe those vents lead into the lab."

Using advanced computer modeling to enhance the sonar data stream echoed back to satellite transducers, Tokaido had also drawn a rough floor plan of the second story.

"There's a stand-alone suite next to where I think the lab is," he said, tracing with his finger the path Bolan would follow through the air tunnel from the roof to the second floor. He snapped his bubble gum a few times in quick succession before adding, "Private bathroom. Porcelain has a great sonar signature."

On missions too numerous to count, Bolan had bet his life on the accuracy of information provided by Stony Man Farm. There was no reason for him to start doubting Aaron Kurtzman's team now.

2

On hands and knees, Bolan moved swiftly through the pitch-black vent, reaching the first intersection at roughly the spot where Tokaido's diagram had indicated it would be. The air system's intersecting branches came together between floors, meaning Bolan was already past the third, and directly above the second story where the lab was located. When he came to the T in the tunnel he remembered was close to the end, he removed the goggles and put them away, confident there were no IR sensors in the vent. Although he had engaged enemies on many occasions while wearing night-vision gear, the view in IR mode occasionally shimmered and stalled for a split second when the gallium arsenide photocathode tubes refreshed. For that reason, Bolan avoided using them when he thought gunfire was imminent.

From his shirt pocket, he pulled a powerful penlight, switched it on, and, holding it between his front teeth, turned into the vent's left branch. Ahead he could see the outline of an access door Tokaido had told him he thought opened onto a stairwell directly next to the lab. It was the spot where Bolan planned to enter the building proper.

Upon reaching the door, he found it was neither secured

nor grated, enabling him to turn the latch from the inside and swing the hatch open. Dropping silently onto the landing, he switched off and put away the penlight, and while walking to the stairwell entrance, drew his Beretta 93-R. Taking a deep breath, he turned the knob with his free hand and opened the door on silent hinges.

A wide hallway with a shiny white linoleum floor stretched the entire length of the second floor, dimly illuminated by track lighting running along the ceiling. On both sides of the corridor, two or three doors were located at various points on otherwise blank windowless walls. One was guarded.

Approximately ten yards away, two men dressed in gray jumpsuits were sitting outside a door on which a security slot similar to those used for hotel rooms was mounted above the latch. As he stepped into the hallway, Bolan's mind registered two critical facts—each man was wearing a lanyard with a magnetic key card clipped to the end and, within easy reach, two Herstal P-90 submachine guns with thirty-round banana clips extending from their ammo ports leaned against the wall. Before Bolan had progressed three steps, one of the men lunged for his weapon.

The Beretta 93-R whispered instant death, delivering a 9 mm Parabellum round that slammed into the side of the man's face before exiting through the back of his skull in a rush of brain tissue and blood that sprayed a fan-shaped pattern of pink droplets onto the white linoleum. The other guard, apparently realizing that the intruder held a lethal advantage, raised his hands over his head and gazed at Bolan with calm eyes.

He was young, perhaps in his late twenties, with pale blue eyes and a pockmark in the middle of his forehead. Across his right cheek, a deep maroon port-wine stain ran from his temple to the line of his jaw.

"Do you speak English?" Bolan asked.

"*Oui*. Yes."

"Where's Dr. Zagorski?" Bolan asked.

The man's eyes shifted for a split second in answer to the question before he replied, "I don't know."

"Are you ready to die?"

"Yes," the young man said.

Bolan motioned with his pistol, said, "Open the door, or I'll kill you and do it myself with your key card."

Without hesitation, the man obeyed, using the magnetic card at the end of his lanyard to gain access.

The door opened into a cavernous modern facility approximately fifty feet square with vented work stations in every corner, large pieces of scientific equipment along the side walls, and an array of laboratory glassware that filled a series of shelves constructed from floor-to-ceiling against the back wall. Numerous beakers, flasks and spiral pipettes of various sizes were arranged on black slate-topped tables throughout the lab, creating the impression that an entire team of scientists was in the midst of conducting research.

A doorless frame leading into a free-standing room in the far corner of the lab was in the general area where Tokaido had told him there might be a stand-alone apartment, presumably for Dr. Zagorski.

As soon as Bolan heard the door close behind him, he rapped the guard at the base of his neck with the Beretta's hand grip. The man exhaled heavily and went down like a sack of grain.

"Dr. Zagorski!" Bolan called out as he slipped a nylon tie wrap around the guard's wrists, securing them behind his back.

A woman dressed in a dark blue night robe appeared in the open door frame, her disheveled reddish-brown hair testifying to the fact that she had been roused from sleep. Despite her rumpled appearance, Bolan recognized her immediately from the photos Hal Brognola had shown him at their initial meeting.

"Get me a weapon," she said before dashing back into the room.

Bolan opened the door and grabbed one of the guards' P-90 submachine guns leaning against the wall. As he was pulling back into the lab, the stairwell door he had used flew open, and four or five men dressed in identical gray jumpsuits charged forward, their automatic rifles spitting lead. Tossing the P-90 behind him into the lab, Bolan returned fire with his Beretta, catching the lead man in the chest with a 3-round burst. The steel-jacketed 9 mm rounds hammered him backward into the path of his oncoming comrades, who threw themselves to the floor in order to get out of the intruder's line of fire.

Sonia Zagorski, fully dressed in jeans, running shoes and a forest green windbreaker with large flapped pockets in the front, ran to Bolan's side as he slammed the door.

"Push this up against it," she said, motioning to one of the heavy slate-topped work stations.

The ten-foot, four hundred pound unit was on casters, enabling them to position it against the door before locking the wheels in place.

"That won't hold them for long," she said while grabbing the P-90 from where it lay on the lab floor. Leaning over the fallen guard, who remained unconscious and breathing heavily, she relieved him of three full banana clips, shoving them into one of her windbreaker's front pockets.

"Help me drag him over to the wall," she said, grabbing the guard by a handful of fabric at the top of his shoulder. "He doesn't have to die."

Bolan nodded and they quickly shoved the limp man against the wall next to the door where he'd be away from the hail of bullets that was sure to commence momentarily.

"Do you have rope?" Zagorski asked, as if she was leading Bolan.

"Can you use that?" he replied, motioning to the submachine gun while pulling the grappling hook and cord from its pouch.

The attractive doctor, in whose hands a P-90 submachine gun looked out of place, deftly slid the bolt to the rear and released it, chambering the magazine's first round.

"Let's go," she said, flipping the safety to its off position as the door began to disintegrate under a barrage of automatic fire from the guards on the other side.

The smell of cordite seeped into the lab to mix with the rising stink of combat and death, while the air filled with the chilling chatter of automatic weapons. The laboratory door started shattering in the center panel above the workbench, the hole growing wider under a steady torrent of bullets.

A gap appeared in the section above the slate-topped table, through which Bolan could see two men firing P-90s on full-auto. He responded with his Desert Eagle, the oversize handgun roaring in the lab's enclosed space with earpopping concussions as he hit the first gunman squarely in the chest. The heavy slug lifted him clean off his feet before slamming him into the wall on the other side of the corridor. He hung in place for a moment as if he had been tacked there by a giant entomologist, then slid slowly to the floor, leaving a messy red streak in his wake.

In the microsecond before the other guard had a chance to dive for cover, Bolan again squeezed the trigger. The round struck the guard in his chest inches below where he cradled the FNH submachine into his shoulder, exiting through a shattered shoulder blade. A spewing jet that included a handful of shredded tissue that moments earlier had been a section of the man's beating heart splattered the distant wall. The force twirled him erratically out of control, his finger frozen in a death grip on the P-90's trigger as he spun to the floor. For a few instants until his clip was exhausted and the firing pin clicked onto an open chamber, steel-tipped bullets flew randomly in all directions, the ones entering the lab ricocheting wildly off slate panels and scientific equipment before embedding themselves in the walls or ceiling.

Hot lead continued slicing the air, the altering trajectories of rounds whizzing through the opening in the door reflective of the shifting positions assumed by the gunmen outside as they scrambled to stay away from Bolan's deadly line of fire.

Although their enemies' efforts had so far been largely ineffective, the rounds flying through the laboratory like angry wasps were life-threatening to both Bolan and Zagorski. The situation was not progressing in their favor, and from all indications, it would get worse if they stayed where they were.

As if in response to Bolan's thoughts, Zagorski leveled her submachine gun at the window and let loose with a 30-round clip while tracing the frame's outline where it connected to the castle's rock walls. The window was clearly a recent addition to the laboratory space, a wooden prefab unit that crumbled outward as neatly and cleanly as if it had been demolished by a team of licensed masons. The resultant wreckage sprayed a cascade of wood splinters and glass shards onto the narrow space between the monastery and the woods where Bolan had hidden the roving guards' bodies, littering the tight area with deadly debris.

The window opening began receiving fire from down below, lethal lead adding to an increasing stream of bullets flying into the lab through the damaged door. Zagorski shoved the barrel of her weapon out the window, and without aiming fired her ammo in a steady burst that swept the area, forcing the guards to seek cover. When her first magazine was empty, she released the spent clip and in one fluid motion, grabbed a 30-rounder from her jacket pocket and shoved it into place while stealing a glance at Bolan. With one hand, he was securing the grappling hook to a heating pipe he was sure would support their weight, while with the other, he fired occasional rounds from the Desert Eagle to keep the guards on the other side of the door from mounting a charge.

Zagorski pressed herself as tightly as possible into the lower corner of where the window had been. Taking advantage of firing from a higher position than her enemies, she began practicing the very same elements of combat discipline Bolan had taught to hundreds of infantry soldiers around the world.

With the patience of a cat waiting for a chipmunk to emerge from under a log where it had disappeared five minutes earlier, Zagorski kept the edge of the barrel barely inside the room, out of sight from those on the ground while she peeked over the edge of the sill. One of the men below let his panic get the better of him and made a dash for what he perceived to be a more advantageous position. Zagorski engaged him with a well-aimed 3-round burst.

The gun's sights had not been battle zeroed for her specific aim, causing the rounds she fired to fly almost a foot to the front and left of where she thought they would hit. The guard froze for a millisecond as he realized he was under attack, giving Zagorski the time she needed to realize the differential in the rifle's sights. She immediately took corrective action by aiming slightly behind her target before letting fly with another quick burst of lead.

In the exact instant the stutter-stepping soldier dived for cover behind a gnarled clump of exposed maple tree roots, Zagorski's rounds entered his lower back at a downward trajectory. The relatively flimsy 5.7 mm bullets traveled through his body in much the same way 5.56 mm NATO rounds could enter a man's shoulder and exit through his thigh by tumbling along the skeletal frame while ripping through soft tissue. Zagorski's rounds struck her victim at the base of his spine and moved upward, with at least one of them exiting through his neck as the combined force of the bullets shoved him violently to the ground.

Zagorski quickly pulled back behind the cover of the wall and scooted below the window to the other side of the opening while checking to make sure the ammo remaining in her magazine was adequate. Taking a deep breath and a few seconds to calm her nerves, she visualized where the other men had been in the split second when almost all her concentration had been on her target.

With the force of a coiled spring, she leaped upright, firing into the spot she had visualized. The tactic worked perfectly. A man standing behind a thin tree with a sawed-off shotgun held to his shoulder was staring at the opposite side of the window opening where Zagorski had been moments earlier. Unfortunately for him, the stubby barrels glinting a shiny blue in the moonlight never got a chance to deliver their payload. Before the gunman realized he was a split second behind his adversary, Zagorski's finger had already squeezed off two 3-round bursts while tracking slightly to the right.

In addition to stitching a straight line through the sapling causing its trunk to crack and split, her steel-jacketed triplets sliced through the gunman's neck, all but decapitating him as he dropped the shotgun and fell three feet into the bushes, arms windmilling in a final release of nervous energy.

Outside, all was suddenly silent.

Dr. Zagorski slung the FNH P-90 submachine gun the way her female colleagues might carry a handbag. By securing the stock under her right arm, she could direct the gun's barrel across a space with the sweep of her forearm as if the rifle was an extension of her hand. This one-armed technique freed her other hand to enable a descent while ensuring she'd retain the ability to fire her weapon on the way down.

As Zagorski stepped to the opening where the window had been and grabbed on to the thin cord with her free hand while wrapping her legs around the line, Bolan pulled two M-18 smoke canisters from his web belt, released their safety latches and tossed the canisters out the window. Within seconds, the area was immersed in thick clouds of billowing smoke as dense and concealing as the worst ocean fogs that occasionally drove ships off course in the North Atlantic.

"Northwest corner of the vineyard!" Bolan shouted into Zagorski's ear a second before she disappeared into the thick smoke that clung in an impervious cloud along the side of the building.

Bolan stood with one foot on the windowsill, about to follow the doctor to the ground forty feet below. With the smoke from the M-18s providing adequate cover, and Zagorski's demonstrated ability with the submachine gun, the soldier was confident that the odds for survival had shifted in their favor.

The damaged workbench, weakened by the riddling absorbed from hundreds of rounds that had shredded the door, suddenly burst ten feet into the laboratory with the force of a runaway locomotive. Guards with automatic weapons spitting death were close behind, using the workbench and door they were forcing forward into the room in much the same way infantry troops use an armored tank to lead the way into an area entrenched by the enemy.

In the back of his mind, Bolan could hear the intermittent staccato bursts of Zagorski's P-90 and realized she was capitalizing on her downward movement through the smoke. Having been in that situation many times himself, he knew Zagorski could use the ground troops' muzzle-flashes, made visible by the thick smoke, as targets. As long as she engaged them with short bursts and continued her downward rappel, her own position would not be betrayed. Bolan also knew that inches above her head, rounds would be sparking and ricocheting against the stone wall where moments earlier, she had been.

Straddling the windowsill with the arm holding his Beretta wrapped around the thin grappling cord, Bolan directed his Desert Eagle at the imploding door and workbench and began pulling the trigger. The combat inexperience of the three guards who were pushing forward behind the workbench was evidenced by the way they aimed their fire directly to their front rather than in wide-sweeping arcs, as if their task was to clear a walking path through dense foliage. Their guns chattered without pause, spraying a steady stream of 5.7 mm rounds, demolishing glassware and work stations, filling the space inside the lab with flying debris.

From his position slightly to the left of the attackers, Bolan fired a rapid quartet from his Desert Eagle, the throaty retort of the .44 Magnum pistol roaring like an angry beast, its heavy bass voice overpowering the lighter pops of the P-90s with tympanic explosions that pulsed against Bolan's eardrums.

The Desert Eagle's steel-jacketed slugs stopped the initial guards cold, tossing the leading two backward as violently as if they had been stuntmen with hydraulic ropes attached to their backs. Bolan's third shot hit a charging gunman square in the chin, the bullet shattering his jawbones like cheap crystal before smashing into the man's chest. The slug exited through his lower back, leaving a fist-size hole that spurted a crimson stream of blood as he fell to the floor.

Bolan leaned out the window, continuing to engage his enemies as they charged into the lab. Bullets snapped the air a finger's width from his face as he prepared to drop to the ground. A guard with his gun on full-auto appeared beyond the shattered door, swinging his weapon's muzzle toward Bolan. The soldier shot him in the upper torso a split second before the FNH rounds hit home. As the dead guard fell backward, he continued firing, sewing a parabolic pattern of 5.7 mm stitches up the wall and across half the ceiling.

Bolan had stemmed the initial attack, but he fully expected another assault to come as soon as the door fortifications completely collapsed. While continuing to fire his Desert Eagle into the laboratory until the bolt clicked open onto an empty chamber, he swung himself outside into the smoky cloud. Without reloading, the combat veteran shoved the oversize handgun into his hip holster while plucking one of the concussion grenades from the suspenders on his web belt.

Aware that the lab was about to fill when his enemies mounted their next counterattack, he set the fuse on the grenade to a 6-second delay before tossing the explosive into the glass-filled room. As he watched the apple-size orb bounce across the white linoleum tiles toward the back wall with its floor-to-ceiling shelves stocked with laboratory glassware, his peripheral vision registered five or six men pushing through the clutter surrounding the door opening. Their muzzle-flashes were visible through the smoke that had drifted from the window opening into the lab to mix with the already copious supply of gun smoke that choked the air. Moments before releasing himself into the night for his slide to earth, Bolan grabbed his Beretta 93-R and sent a delaying burst into the fray, adding a final contribution to the overpowering stench of burning cordite and flesh.

During the entire two and a half seconds he free fell, with hot lead whizzing by his face making the time seem like an eternity, Bolan instinctively knew at every moment exactly how far above the ground he was. At the last possible instant, he snapped the hand holding the grappling cord, causing his descent to come to an immediate halt. As he released the thin line and stepped onto the ground, he drew his Desert Eagle and rammed a fresh magazine into its ammo port.

Fifty feet above, the concussion grenade detonated with an air-expanding blast followed a nanosecond later by a deadly blizzard of shredded glass that spewed out the window with the force of a Gulf Coast hurricane. A horrific medley of angry cries and painful shrieks erupted as a black cloud of toxic smoke poured from the building.

With handguns drawn, Bolan struck off on a course through the woods that would get him to the road in two or three minutes. From there, he'd have a short run to the corner of the vineyard where he hoped Dr. Zagorski would be waiting by the all-terrain vehicles. The foliage was sparse, with none of the clinging vines or heavy vegetation he had encountered on so many other hellfire trails around the world, and he reached the edge of the woods without incident.

When he came to the road, Bolan paused for a second to gauge the degree of his enemies' resistance. Occasional bursts of sporadic automatic fire could be heard coming from below, but the pattern of gunshots was not indicative of an organized assault or defense. Hal Brognola had thought there were fewer than two dozen armed guards at the monastery. A quick calculation told Bolan that he and Zagorski had already dispatched approximately half that number.

Most of the smoke from the M-18 canisters had dissipated, but the residual tendrils, in combination with the inky black night, severely limited visibility as the soldier ran down the curvy road. Pulling his goggles over his eyes and switching into IR mode, he was able to quickly pick out Dr. Zagorski as she zigzagged like a running back sprinting toward the goal line.

Approximately twenty yards behind her, two guards were firing their submachine guns in her direction, their hot barrels glowing incandescently through Bolan's IR-enriched lenses. With the hand holding his Beretta, he thumbed the selector switch, aligning the arrow with the three white dots.

Without breaking stride, he sent a triburst of 9 mm rounds into the head and neck of one guard while simultaneously firing his Desert Eagle at the other. His action drew reciprocal gunfire from a guard ten yards or so farther down the road, causing Bolan to immediately adopt a zigzagging pattern similar to Zagorski while he engaged the gunners.

With both hands dispatching death, Bolan sprinted through an IR-illuminated shooting gallery, the deep-voiced roar of his hefty Desert Eagle drowning out the lighter patter of the Order of Raphael's weapons.

By the time Bolan caught up to Zagorski, they were close to the bottom of the hill. The only concealment available was from the flimsy cloak of darkness.

Holstering his weapons, the Executioner jumped onto the wired all-terrain vehicle, yelling for Zagorski to get on behind him. While she was climbing onto the wide seat, they came under fire from a position close to the stairs leading up the hill to the monastery. When Bolan flipped the ignition switch and the ATV leaped to life, Zagorski returned fire, hosing the area at the base of the hill with a steady stream of rounds until her magazine ran dry.

Her rounds found their mark, causing the guard to dance and jerk. She released the spent clip, replacing it with the final one she had taken from the fallen guard in the lab. Bolan plied the throttle, propelling them at breakneck speed through the vineyard between two rows of vines, leaving the noise of battle behind.

Bolan gunned the ATV's engine while keeping his eyes on the skyline where the darker density of the woods bordering the vineyard converged with the night sky. He was searching for a specific spot along the top of the trees where the peaks of four centuries-old maples came together, pointing inward to form an easily recognizable pyramid pattern. They were drawing close, and he eased up on the throttle.

"What?" Zagorski yelled, her eyes probing the darkness for enemies.

"We're close to the car."

His eyes scanned the intersection of sky and trees as they proceeded forward.

"Here!"

He braked to an abrupt stop, flipped the power toggle switch to its off position and dismounted.

"Come on," he shouted over his shoulder as he began crossing through the rows of vines. "Watch the wire," he added, referring to the zinc cable running the entire length of each row.

When they passed through the final set of vines and reached a paved road between the vineyard and woods, Bolan ran directly across to a small stand of scrub pines where a silver Porsche 911 Turbo gleamed dully in the night. Zagorski was steps behind, carrying her submachine gun at port arms as she ran to the passenger door.

The instant Bolan's fingers wrapped around the driver's door handle, the car's rear-mounted engine came to life, purring powerfully under the curved frame. He increased his pressure on the handle, and Zagorski's door unlocked and swung open. She jumped in, holding her gun at an angle between her legs, with the hot barrel inches from the window.

"Who are you?" she asked as her door closed and Bolan pressed the accelerator to the floor.

The Porsche fishtailed out of the woods onto the paved highway, leaping forward like a pouncing panther when its tires met the tar surface. Bolan upshifted quickly through the powerful automobile's second and third gears, swiftly accelerating to a speed in excess of 120 miles an hour as they zipped on a path as straight as an arrow down the highway, leaving the ancient L'Abbaye de Raphael in the rearview mirror.

"We'll be at the tunnel in less than five minutes," was all Bolan said.

Zagorski nodded, knowing he was referring to a mile-long tunnel under a section of foothills that rose to become the Pyrenees Mountains separating France from Spain. The customs checkpoint, where according to Brognola, Bolan's vehicle would already be cleared for a direct nonstop drive through, was another five miles down the road.

"Thank you, whoever you are. They were going to kill me." Zagorski paused, swallowed hard and added in a voice more appropriate for a confessional than the interior of a sports car, "The work they made me do is evil. I tried to go as slowly as I could."

"You did okay," Bolan replied, keeping his eyes glued to the front. "There's a plane waiting for us in San Sebastian."

The road was wide and smooth, with two lanes in each direction separated by a center median in which a row of red maples had been planted at intervals of approximately twenty feet. At the speed they were traveling, the small trees whizzing past in Bolan's peripheral vision took on the appearance of a continuous hedge.

When they reached an area in the foothills where the road turned curvy, Bolan downshifted into the first S-curve while checking the rearview mirror.

"You think they're coming after us?" Zagorski asked. "You keep looking into the mirror."

"We don't want to be surprised," he answered as he accelerating into the curve, then quickly downshifted as they raced into the next bend. Displaying the timing and reflexes of a race car driver, Bolan alternated between downshifting and accelerating, negotiating one hairpin turn after another at speeds that caused the vehicles's high-performance tires to smoke and squeal in protest. When he entered the last S-turn ending in a straightaway that covered the final half mile leading into the tunnel, two lights characteristic in size and shape of those designed on the front fuselage of a Bell 206 helicopter jumped into his rearview mirror.

The chopper was incoming fast, at close to twice Bolan's speed, closing the gap between them at a rate that would place the aircraft on top of the Porsche before it reached the tunnel.

Bolan slammed his foot onto the brake and jerked the steering wheel to the left, causing the sports car to slide into a tire-smoking sideways skid that painted wide rubber stripes down the center of the highway.

The helicopter pilot was not anticipating Bolan's maneuver, and he whizzed straight past, strafing the road inches in front of the Porsche's reinforced bumper. The .20-caliber machine-gun rounds blazing from the helicopter's underside left deep pockmarks in the highway's smooth surface.

As Bolan straightened his car and accelerated toward the tunnel's entrance, the pilot pulled the nose of his aircraft upward, attempting to perform a complete reverse turn before his prey was able to reach the safety of the passageway. The pilot's desire to align his chopper with the highway told Bolan that the machine gun was on a fixed mount. The configuration required the pilot to work with his gunner in order to get the barrel pointed generally in the right direction, a fact Bolan used to his advantage. He stomped the accelerator, and the silver sports car took off like a rocket, pressing both passengers into the plush leather seats as it sped into the safety of the mile-long tunnel.

Coming in from the dark, the brightness of the tungsten lights mounted into the ceiling made Bolan squint. There were no other vehicles in sight, and he eased off the gas pedal to give himself a few extra seconds of safety to consider his next move.

"They'll send someone in to chase us out," Zagorski said in a low quavering voice that made Bolan wonder if she had reached her point of exhaustion. After her performance at the monastery, he wouldn't fault her if she had. "And the helicopter will be waiting."

Unbeknown to her, an M-72 66 mm Light Antitank Weapon was sitting ready for use in the vehicle's front trunk. The problem Bolan pondered was how to deploy the weapon in this particular situation. The tube in which the LAW's missile was assembled was open at both ends, which meant the user had to account for a backblast. When the missile ignited, it sent a dangerous tongue of flame and hot gases six feet to the rear.

"We can open the roof, and I'll fire at them as soon as we come out of the tunnel," Zagorski said, shifting the P-90 she held at an angle between her knees.

"Not good odds," Bolan replied. "Not with a Bell. There's too much plate on the belly for your rounds."

Spotting a pair of taillights ahead, he accelerated to catch up. As he got close, he saw it was a pickup truck at least ten years old, the faded paint dented and scratched in numerous places.

"We just got lucky," Bolan said as he steered into the passing lane and tapped his gas pedal to pull even with the pickup. One of the hubcaps on the driver's side was missing, and the metal sides around the open cargo area were pocked with large sections of maroon rust. The rocker panels had rusted completely through in so many places they appeared to be made of red lace.

"Get him to stop," Bolan said, pressing the switch to lower Zagorski's window.

She shouted in French to the driver, a man who looked to be in his midsixties, who first stared at her, shook his head, then stared straight forward, his hands gripping the steering wheel tightly enough to turn his gnarled knuckles white.

Bolan moved forward until the Porsche was halfway beyond the truck before he inched the steering wheel to the right, easing the car's back fender panel into the pickup's front bumper.

The old man started shouting and gesturing with universally understood hand signals, but with sparks flying from where the two vehicles were rubbing together, and with the vast superiority the Porsche held over the old pickup, he was forced out of the lane onto a narrow breakdown shoulder barely wide enough for a car to sit beyond the traffic's flow.

When they had come to a complete halt with the Porsche blocking the pickup's path, Bolan said, "Come with me," threw his door open and jumped out. Upon reaching the truck, he reached up and pulled the driver's door open.

The old man continued shouting and gesturing wildly until his eyes glanced at the Desert Eagle in Bolan's left hand. Under the bright tungsten lighting, the huge handgun gleamed with evil purpose.

Zagorski stared at the gun with eyes as large as saucers, apparently as apprehensive as the truck driver that Bolan was about to shoot him.

"Tell him not to be afraid."

Zagorski translated quickly, but her voice as well as the old man's face belied their belief in Bolan's words. It was obvious they were both terrified.

"Buy his truck. Fifty thousand euros," Bolan stated in a voice that held no room for negotiation. "The cash is in the glove compartment."

Zagorski related the message, which, because it amounted to approximately one hundred thousand U.S. dollars, was not believed. The man's bottom lip was trembling, and his hands shook as if he was afflicted with palsy. His eyes remained glued to the Desert Eagle.

"Get the money. Hurry," Bolan said.

Zagorski ran the few steps back to the car, reached in through her open window and came back with a wad of high-denomination bills.

"Tell him again. Fifty thousand euros."

The sight of the money brought a smile to the old man's face. In this part of the world, populated along an international border with a culture bred of an interesting combination including ancient Christianity, Islam and Basque, men did not pass judgment on the business of others. Within the local value system, a smuggler or drug dealer could conduct legitimate transactions as subsets of an overall illicit plan without necessarily involving a third party in anything illegal or immoral. Regardless of Bolan's business, he was offering a transaction the old man found very easy to view as legitimate.

The old man asked for the Porsche as well.

Zagorski couldn't help but smile as she translated the request.

"No," Bolan answered. "It's not mine. Someone will come by to pick it up."

A slight smile touched at the corners of his mouth for a

second as he imagined Hal Brognola explaining to the President that one of the CIA's high-technology special mission models complete with armor plating, bulletproof glass, and a 5.56 mm machine gun concealed above the tailpipe, was being used to run errands into town by an old hay farmer in Southern France.

"No," he said again.

The man nodded, and, with his smile exposing a mouthful of crowded, crooked teeth, took the stack of bills from Zagorski and shoved them into his pocket. Despite the fact he was bareheaded, he made a motion of tipping his cap to both Zagorski and Bolan, and set off walking back the way they had come in.

"You drive," Bolan said, pointing to the truck as he returned to the Porsche.

Zagorski climbed into the pickup and backed it away, allowing Bolan to ease the Porsche against the wall of the tunnel to keep it as far as possible out of the traffic lane until someone could retrieve it.

After shutting down the engine, Bolan released the latch to open the car's front trunk compartment revealing the LAW.

"Who are you?" Zagorski asked again as Bolan grabbed the LAW and pulled on both ends to expand the weapon. The inner tube telescoped outward to the rear, guided by a channel assembly that housed the firing pin and detent lever. Once the detent was aligned under the trigger bar locking the inner tube in its extended position, the LAW was cocked and ready.

"A man with options," Bolan answered while wrapping his free hand around the driver's door handle to activate the car's sophisticated antitampering system. The Porsche's passenger window slid closed as Bolan hopped into the back of the pickup and settled himself into a kneeling position.

There were half a dozen holes in the cargo bed's floor through which he could see the pavement moving by as Zagorski pulled out of the breakdown shoulder into the travel lane. As he visualized the helicopter awaiting their exit from the tunnel, Bolan shifted his position so he would be facing the rear, making sure he left adequate space between himself and the back of the cab for the missile's backblast.

Bolan reasoned that the chopper would be hovering on top of the tunnel's opening, its position placing it behind and above an exiting vehicle. The gunsights would be properly aligned with the highway, waiting for the target to appear. To his advantage, Bolan didn't think his enemies would be expecting his getaway vehicle to be a dilapidated old truck. He figured he'd have two or three seconds to position the LAW's front reticle sight onto the aircraft and press the rubber-enclosed trigger bar on top of the outer tube to fire the missile. Three seconds after exit was the best he could hope for—by then, the pilot and gunman would realize a man was kneeling in the back of a pickup with the business end of a shoulder-fired rocket launcher pointed their way. They would have but one response for that.

Zagorski pressed the truck's gas pedal to the floor. The vehicle gained speed, gradually reaching its top velocity of slightly less than forty miles per hour. Ahead, the mouth of the tunnel appeared as a pitch black circle leading into the night.

As they drew close, Bolan flipped the reticle sight into its upright position, positioned the LAW on his right shoulder and lightly placed his fingers over the rubber-encased bar.

The LAW's reticle sight was a piece of Plexiglas with an image resembling a V etched into the heavy plastic. The weapon was designed to assign the correct distance and elevation to the missile if the operator was able to place his target exactly within the lines of the V. If parts of the target extended outside the V reticle, which was graduated in twenty-five meter range increments, the missile would launch long and usually strike above the intended impact point. Too much space between the target and the walls of the V would result in a short shot.

With the LAW's maximum effective range of 660 feet, Bolan hoped the helicopter would be hovering low over the highway. The lower the chopper, the better his chances to hit it with a less-than-perfect aim.

The steady sound of the Bell's blades could be heard when the truck was ten yards or so from the exit. Bolan's assessments of his enemy's positioning and intended tactics had apparently both been correct, and he took a deep breath, letting it out slowly to steady himself.

As the pickup moved through the exit into the dark night, he noticed an area on the highway roughly fifty yards outside the tunnel that was illuminated by a powerful spotlight mounted on the chopper's underside. Before they reached that spot, Bolan realized, he'd have to fire the LAW's missile.

The instant his line of vision cleared the edge of the tunnel, allowing him to see the sky, Bolan placed the hovering Bell 206 into the center of the reticle's V sight. The helicopter was low, perhaps no more than two hundred feet off the ground, when he depressed the trigger bar and felt the missile on his shoulder come to life. With an eardrum-aching *whoosh* and a backblast of fire and hot gases, the high-explosive armor-piercing warhead zipped out the front of the LAW, crashing straight into the belly of the hovering aircraft.

Before the gunner had time to squeeze even one round from his gun, the helicopter exploded in a fireball that illuminated the countryside in orange light. Resembling an outer-space creature in a poorly produced science-fiction movie, the mangled mass of burning machinery tumbled onto the top of the tunnel exit, where it balanced for a moment before crashing onto the highway.

The thunderous sounds of two secondary explosions that scattered pieces of sizzling helicopter metal across both travel lanes echoed across the rolling terrain. With the echo of the blast ringing in his ears, Bolan reached into a pouch on his web belt, withdrew a cell phone, and speed-dialed a secure number.

"Yes?" Hal Brognola answered an ocean away, the sleep in his voice reminding Bolan that in the nation's capital, people had been in bed for only a few hours.

"Customs," Bolan said. "Three minutes. Not the Turbo. Blue pickup truck, two passengers."

"Good job, Striker," Brognola replied.

He hung up without another word. There would be plenty of time for talk when they got to Stony Man Farm.

3

Less than twenty-four hours after returning from his mission to L'Abbaye de Raphael in Bayonne, Mack Bolan sat with Hal Brognola at a conference table in the War Room at Stony Man Farm. Also with them was Aaron Kurtzman's cybernetics team, consisting of the methodical, common sense Carmen Delahunt, Huntington Wethers, a distinguished former college professor who brought an academic, facts-based approach to research, and Akira Tokaido, a natural hacker whose innate skills could have enabled him to be one of the best professional gamers in the world had he not chosen instead to serve his country as a member of the Stony Man team. Together, they were a case study for synergy, often arriving at solutions via insights far greater than the sum of the supporting data.

"Nice job on the schematics," Bolan said across the table to Tokaido.

Tokaido acknowledged the compliment by snapping his bubble gum three times in rapid succession before replying derisively, "They were just 3-D."

From more than six feet away, Bolan could hear a tinny percussive sound coming from the young man's high-fidelity earbuds, and wondered for more than the hundredth time how he could hear and respond to normal conversation amid the racket accosting his eardrums from the MP3 player he carried in his shirt pocket.

"Zagorski has been debriefed?" Bolan asked Brognola, who was dressed in a navy blue suit with a button-down white shirt starched so heavily it looked as if it could be made of cardboard.

"Yes. But let's wait until Kurtzman gets here."

As if on cue, the doors to the elevator built into the corner of the room slid open, and Barbara Price, Stony Man's mission controller, appeared, followed by Aaron Kurtzman, who wheeled himself to his place at the head of the conference table. As Price slid into a vacant seat next to Tokaido, Kurtzman took his oversize mug of steaming coffee and placed it on the table in front of him.

"Hal, Zagorski's debrief," he said without wasting any words on greetings.

"It's not good," the big Fed replied. "As we suspected, the Order of Raphael is definitely working to develop a bio-weapon. In the three years between 1345 and 1348, the Black Death wiped out somewhere between thirty and fifty percent of Europe's population. Zagorski thinks the Order actually stored blood taken from plague victims during the fourteenth century in wine bottles in one of their cellars. They began those experiments that caught the attention of Sentinelles hoping to resurrect the disease, but the blood was too old. They decided instead to create a modern pandemic from scratch."

"Motivation?" Bolan asked.

"I can answer that," Price spoke up. In addition to the skills she brought to her management responsibilities, the former model with honey-blond hair was an adept researcher. She was knowledgeable and incisive, but even she admitted that her mind lacked that special ability to make the type of quantum leaps the cybernetics team often achieved when they pooled their mental resources.

"The Order dates all the way back to before the Crusades," Price said. "When Pope Clement moved the papal seat to Avignon and it looked like there would be a schism with Rome, L'Abbaye de Raphael, along with all the other French monasteries, became more prominent in Church affairs. They're mentioned in many medieval documents, but it's hard to tell where truth leaves off and a rather incredible legend begins. Some believe that the Order's calling was to help enforce God's punishments on man."

When Price paused for a moment, Wethers said, "Vigilante monks killing sinners?" His voice held a note of skepticism.

He placed the ivory stem of a briar pipe between his teeth and leaned back in his chair, taking on a pose multitudes of students had observed whenever the African-American professor assumed what he called his Socratic mode of teaching.

"Not exactly," Price answered. "More like facilitators. The Old Testament is very explicit concerning God's quid pro quo relationship with his Chosen People. Sinning gets out of control, and He sends a flood, choosing Noah to work with Him to punish mankind. Avenging angels are sent to destroy Sodom and Gomorra. Moses is tasked to impose a forty-year cleansing march onto the doubting children of Israel. The legend is that the Order of Raphael was chosen to help spread the plague throughout Europe. Supposedly, a task force called the Forty Martyrs infected themselves and went on their way, spreading the disease along with God's gospel. In those times, monks and priests were one of few groups allowed free travel across international borders."

"Why forty?" Delahunt, ever the addict for attention to detail, asked.

"One for each lash Jesus received. But they weren't all dispatched at once. The story goes that the Order sent them out in pairs and trios over a three-year period when the plague devastated European populations the Order's abbot constantly watched for a sign telling him when to deploy the final couriers of death, steadfastly believing God would let him know. The plague ended up manifesting itself in three variants—bubonic, with black tumors and death within two weeks, pneumatic, zeroing in on the respiratory system, spread merely by breathing on someone and fatal in days, and finally, the septicemic version, of which the initial symptom was a violent vomiting of blood with death occurring within hours. The appearance of the third mutation, interpreted by the Order's abbot to symbolize the Trinity, was his signal to deploy the last group. The plague died out shortly thereafter."

"Are you saying that the explanation we learned in school, that the Black Death was spread by fleas carried on rats, is false?" Bolan asked.

"I'm just telling you what the legend is, Striker," Price said.

"Why did the plague stop spreading? Rats didn't change their travel patterns," Tokaido asked.

"Darwinian natural selection," Wethers answered in his authoritarian voice. "People possessing a natural resistance survived, and as those contracting the disease died, potential victims became fewer and fewer. Almost half the population in some places was wiped out."

"In Europe," Tokaido countered. "Rats didn't migrate off the continent?" He snapped his gum and added, "Probability of the legend being fact is not zero."

"Akira's right," Delahunt said. "Assume the Order was the breakout epicenter, targeting only the Christian world for God's punishment. They stop sending couriers and the disease dies out. Coincidence? There must have been susceptible people in places like the Ottoman Empire, which bordered the continent. Why was the disease confined almost exclusively to Europe?"

At the head of the table, Kurtzman smiled with pride at the way his cybernetics team could creatively brainstorm, considering innovative and sometimes ridiculous hypotheses while progressing down a path eventually leading to insight.

"What the Order of Raphael did or did not do centuries ago is not the issue, is it?" he asked, not wanting them to get embroiled in a historical discussion.

"The legend is only for reference," Price answered. "With so many people looking to the Middle East and questioning if certain biblical prophecies are coming true, these men may actually believe they're doing God's work. That makes them very dangerous."

Bolan recalled the way the guard with the port-wine stain on his face had been unafraid of death outside the laboratory in Bayonne.

"How capable are they without Zagorski?" Kurtzman asked, and, eyeing Bolan, added, "I assume they have one fewer functioning laboratory than they did prior to last night?"

Brognola said, "Dr. Zagorski didn't think Bayonne was the only site developing the disease. Apparently the type of virus they're working on needs three components. She thought only one was coming out of the Bayonne lab."

"You said the Order has offices in Sydney and Boston?" Bolan asked, recalling the initial briefing he received on the National Mall.

"Yes. And there's a reporter for the *Boston Tribune* who wrote a series of articles last year about a team of scientists in Australia. They were working to create a genetically engineered virus to attack their cyclical rodent problem and stumbled across a way to make ordinary diseases incredibly potent. They published their results in 1999 in a collection of essays entitled *The New Terror,* which specifically addressed bioweapon terrorism."

"Boston reporter and Sydney scientists. Another coincidence?" Delahunt asked. "I hate coincidences."

"And that's why I think Striker should go to Boston," Brognola answered. "To conduct a soft—" he paused and repeated his words for emphasis "—a *soft* probe of the Order's facility. And while you're there, you can stop by the *Tribune* and talk to this reporter about the Australian team. At the time she conducted her research, years before 9/11 made everything a potential terrorist weapon, they were the world's leading virologists."

"Do you know the name of the lead scientist on that project? I'll have him checked out," Price said.

"Terrance MacPherson," Brognola replied.

Kurtzman took a sip of his coffee and swallowed slowly, savoring the taste of his special blend. "Then it looks like our course is set," he said, indicating the meeting was over.

"One more thing," Brognola said, and the tone in his voice made the team pay attention to his words. "The President wants me to keep a representative from Sentinelles informed. I've met the guy, a doctor named Robert Cafard, and I don't like him, but I will do the President's bidding. He's very concerned about our current relationship with France in light of Iraq and Lebanon."

"Why don't you like him?" Tokaido asked, and before Brognola had a chance to answer, said, "I'll check him out for you."

"You think you can crack French security to get to his really personal records?" Delahunt asked in a teasing voice.

The hacker answered with an appropriate sideways glance in her direction.

"Okay, then," Kurtzman said again. "Our course is set. Let's get to work."

4

The main conference room situated on the top floor of L'Abbaye de Raphael was a bit on the dark side, as was the soul of the current abbot. When elected to his position two years earlier, he had followed a tradition set by all previous abbots in charge of the monastery dedicated to the archangel Raphael and assumed the title "Abbot Gabriel" along with his leadership role. The Order's members had elected a leader they knew would guide them to fulfill their calling in troubled times. Even without the obvious signs broadcast daily from the Middle East, the Order could see that the prophesied end was drawing near. The members had elected a leader they believed received visions from God.

As he sat at the heavy conference table carved by European artisans more than two centuries earlier from a single slab of Black Forest oak, Abbot Gabriel let his gaze wander across the wood-paneled walls. How was it possible that two nights earlier a soldier of the Beast had successfully breached the walls of his abbey, leaving death and destruction in his wake?

Gabriel glanced beyond the thick beveled glass in the windows that gave him a partial view of the vineyard below. His fellow apostles were repairing the all-terrain vehicles the soldier of the Beast had damaged during his midnight assault. With his pulse racing in anger, the abbot pulled his gaze back into the room.

Four deacons sat with him at the table, their faces etched with residual strain from the intruder's attack. The speaker, also one of the Order's deacons, and whose primary responsibility was the monastery's security, finished his presentation assessing the damage and the status of repair, and asked if there were questions.

"Tell me, Brother Matthew, how far behind schedule does losing all of Dr. Zagorski's work put us?" Gabriel asked.

The deacon nodded. "No more than one month. Perhaps much less."

"Explain."

Matthew wiped a few beads of sweat from above his upper lip and said, "Dr. Zagorski's laboratory was under surveillance while she worked. Thus, we have her experiments on videotape. We have her notes and research on the main computer's database. We'll resurrect her research at our Boston site."

Gabriel's elbows were propped on the table, his folded hands held in front of his mouth with the index fingers extended as if he was ready to recite the child's rhyme about a church and steeple. He stared into the distance while pondering the deacon's answer.

"Under surveillance while she worked," he repeated into the belfry of his finger church. "But not during the assault to record an image of the Beast's soldier."

"No. We saw no need to keep the video running around the clock."

Matthew's eyes searched the abbot's face as if seeking encouragement, or perhaps support. He found neither.

Gabriel said, "Nevertheless, I have seen the soldier," and those at the table knew he was referring to one of his visions. "He is an American, and he travels as we speak to Boston. He seeks a woman there. A newspaper reporter. The forces of the Beast have learned about MacPherson."

Brother Thomas, sitting next to Gabriel, spoke. "MacPherson is almost finished. We'll fly his portion to the Caribbean next week and bring it into Boston via ship. Getting it into the United States by air is too risky. In approximately two weeks, we will have all three components at our Boston site."

"And the Forty Martyrs?" Gabriel asked.

"Safe one hour south of Boston. In Newport, Rhode Island. Since they're already in the country; there is no way the American's Homeland Security Department will prevent them from traveling to Boston, New York, Chicago and Los Angeles. From the United States, God's pestilence will spread throughout the world. Our people will not fail."

Gabriel turned slightly in his chair in order to drill Thomas with a direct stare. "Your people better not fail," he said softly in a voice as cold as arctic ice.

Turning back to Matthew, he asked, "How many apostles were taken by the soldier of the Beast?"

"Nineteen."

Gabriel paused for a moment to let his flash of anger subside before he replied, "Blessed are the dead who die in the name of the Lord."

"Amen," the men seated around the table said in unison.

5

Leslie Rodrigues was not a news reporter. Her position at the *Boston Tribune,* which she honestly believed to be the best job in the world, was in the sports department covering the trials and tribulations of the Boston Red Sox. However, two years earlier, while serving in news as part of a requirement for all junior reporters to rotate through the paper's functional departments, she had followed a story that led to a team of Australian scientists who were attempting, through genetic engineering, to create a lethal virus that could ride on existing rodent diseases such as mouse pox.

Their objective was to combat the cyclical population spikes the continent endured every four years when what the Australians refer to as a "plague of mice" overran their country. If successful, the scientists planned to adapt their technology to also battle rabbits and rats, which each year destroy approximately seven billion dollars' worth of crops and grazing land. Instead, they ended up discovering a process to combine common ailments such as the flu with deadly new viruses that could turn an ordinary cold into a fatal disease with no known antidote. While researching her story, Rodrigues reluctantly became the *Tribune*'s expert on the shadowy world of bioweapons.

Mack Bolan knew all this. Before leaving Stony Man Farm, Price had given him a dossier on Leslie Rodrigues cobbled together with data extracted from supposedly secure databases at the newspaper, the Massachusetts Registry of Motor Vehicles and the Internal Revenue Service. Complete with half a dozen recent photographs, the file gave Bolan everything he needed to know about the woman prior to calling her request an appointment.

Her disinclination to set aside time to meet with someone entirely outside the world of sports resulted in a gentle call to her editor from a man in the Justice Department who suggested that the paper might not enjoy enduring a financial audit from the IRS he described as being analogous to a colonoscopy. The editor had apparently been the one to convince Rodrigues that "taking one for the team" by giving a few hours of her time was the prudent course of action. Being a sports reporter, she obviously understood the importance of team play, because a spot in her schedule immediately became available for the man calling himself Matthew Cooper.

Despite it being a Wednesday afternoon, the Boston Public Gardens were crowded. Summer brought a wave of tourists to the historic city, and certain attractions such as the Swan Boats, Fenway Park and Bunker Hill drew visitors from far and wide.

As he threaded his way through the throngs of tourists, residents and students jamming the pedestrian paths crisscrossing the public garden, Mack Bolan was thinking more of the soft probe he planned to conduct that night on the Order of Raphael's Park Drive facility than he was of Leslie Rodrigues. He considered her nothing more than a background source, providing information that might help him understand the complexity of developing a bioweapon, and thus gauge the severity of the Order's threat. His primary mission in Boston was to physically reconnoiter the enemy's outpost.

He was wearing black pants and a dark blue windbreaker with snaps up the front and an expertly tailored section inserted under the left arm to conceal the bulge of a shoulder holster holding his Beretta 93-R. Knowing that if he was forced to use the weapon it would most likely be in a public setting, Bolan had outfitted the pistol with its stubby sound suppressor before leaving his hotel room.

Although he was taking the precaution to be armed, he was not expecting trouble. No one knew he was coming to Boston, traveling under the name Matt Cooper. A genuine Massachusetts driver's license and three credit cards in his wallet, all given to him by Hal Brognola prior to leaving Stony Man Farm, confirmed his identity.

The weather was pleasantly warm and dry, and Bolan enjoyed strolling through the picturesque gardens as he made his way to the appointed rendezvous. Well-tended beds of Asian day lilies filled the air with a cloying fragrance as he walked past, the plantings hugging the gentle curves of the pedestrian paths wide enough for more than a dozen people to stand abreast. Vendors hawked pretzels, drinks, ice cream and candied apples from brightly painted carts placed at random spots throughout the gardens, while performing mimes, jugglers and musicians vied for the loose change in tourists' pockets. Groups of students who chose to remain the entire summer in Boston were scattered throughout the park, enjoying the outdoors as only people of that age, who have no serious responsibilities hanging over their heads, could. The atmosphere was festive, as might be expected on a glorious summer day in a city that housed more universities and colleges than did many states.

Bolan and Rodrigues had agreed to meet on or next to the third bench in front of the entrance to the Swan Boat ride. As he approached, the Executioner drank in the sights and sounds of folks young and old, families as well as singles, enjoying a good time. He savored the all too few days like this when his fellow Americans unwittingly helped him realize why he did what he did.

The soldier's peripheral vision suddenly caught an object speeding through the air toward his head. As he turned to counter it, his right hand reflexively slipped into the front of his windbreaker, coming to rest on the Beretta's hand grip within a microsecond. The threatening projectile was a runaway flying disk that had caught an uplifting current and sailed over the head of a young man who was making a feeble, uncoordinated attempt to turn and get under it. MIT emblazoned in blue block lettering across the front of his white T-shirt made Bolan think that despite being a poor athlete, the kid was probably an ass-kicker when it came to differential calculus.

Bolan snatched the whirling disk from midair with his left hand, and in one continuous motion flicked it back to the student who caught it with both hands and yelled "Thanks" before spinning on his heel. Using a sweeping haymaker technique, he sent the Frisbee on a wobbly flight toward a group of similarly dressed young people who laughed and clapped at their friend's poor performance.

Bolan had entered the public gardens from the Arlington Street gateway, where Commonwealth Avenue came to a dead end after running eight blocks through a serene area called Back Bay. Million-dollar renovated brownstones lined both sides of the street, a roadway comprised of two one-way thoroughfares with three lanes each for traffic going in opposite directions. A grassy median populated with trees and huge bronze statutes of various figures from the city's storied history separated the two.

Immediately inside the entrance to the gardens was a huge bronze statue of George Washington mounted on a gigantic horse. Shortly after passing the first President, who was cast in a pose suggesting he was leading troops into battle, Bolan crossed a small stone bridge spanning a narrow section of the Swan Boat pond. Tourists were gathered in clumps on the bridge where they could watch as the boats carrying loads of laughing children passed beneath. Ever the soldier, Bolan's mind processed the students, the families, the groups of tourists as random obstructions to clear lines of fire should he find himself pressed to use the Beretta strapped tightly against his rock-hard left pectorals.

He arrived at the rendezvous point fifteen minutes early, completing a quick reconnoiter of the area before returning to the designated bench. It was unoccupied, and he took a seat facing the entryway to the boat ride where he could see up and down the path he had traversed. Bolan didn't know which direction Rodrigues would be coming from, and she would not know him by sight. But he had told her what he'd be wearing, and he knew he'd recognize her from the photos Kurtzman had obtained for him.

Less than five minutes later, Bolan spotted the reporter as soon as she crested a small rise in the walkway. She was approximately a hundred yards away, approaching from the opposite direction from where Bolan had entered the gardens. Judging from the fluidity of her smooth purposeful gait, he immediately suspected she was an athlete. Her arms were swinging freely by her sides, and on first glance, she appeared to be an attractive young woman enjoying an afternoon stroll through the park without a care in the world.

It was only when she got close, and she drilled him with her eyes while giving a look that clearly conveyed danger, that Bolan realized something was wrong. A second before he rose from his seat to greet her, he understood her visual message and caught himself. Instead of standing, he leaned back on the bench and glanced away for an instant to dispel any appearance of recognition. Letting his gaze return to her general vicinity, he watched her advance without looking directly at her.

"I'm being followed," she said when she drew close enough to be heard. "Two men, blue-and-white running suits."

She walked straight past the bench without the slightest pause, angling off toward a vending stand selling ice-cream bars. The two men she mentioned came into view, their eyes glued to the woman as they dodged between people crowding the walkway. The way they were working to maintain their distance clearly demonstrated a lack of military training.

Rodrigues stopped at the vendor, made her selection, then strolled to a nearby trash barrel to unwrap the ice-cream sandwich she had bought. The men stopped short when she did, awkwardly shuffling a few feet in one direction and then the other, never taking their eyes from their prey.

Rodrigues, however, proceeded to conduct a maneuver that immediately impressed Bolan. After unwrapping a portion of the ice cream and taking a few small bites, she resumed her walk, stopping at another trash barrel about twenty yards distant to remove and discard the remaining wrapping. She had perfectly calculated the distance her followers were keeping, and her second stop placed them directly in front of Bolan.

The first thing that caught his attention were the diamond-shaped scars on the backs of their left hands. A moonlit image flashed through his mind as he recalled the two roving guards he had killed outside L'Abbaye de Raphael in Bayonne. They had both been marked with similar scars. The second item that registered in his mind was that they were armed. Off-the-rack running suits did little to conceal shoulder holsters from the eyes of someone with enough experience to recognize the characteristic bulge and creases they produced.

Rodrigues resumed walking at a very slow pace, as if eating the ice cream and keeping it from dripping onto the short white skirt she was wearing prevented her from resuming her previous speed. Her followers maintained their distance, and once they were beyond his bench, Bolan rose and walked off the pedestrian path onto the grass so he could trail along less conspicuously on a line parallel to the reporter and her followers.

Rodrigues followed the general route Bolan had taken coming into the gardens, passing over the narrow portion of the pond on the little stone bridge where she stopped for a moment to wave and call out a greeting to the children riding below. When she came to the Washington statue, instead of continuing straight and exiting the Gardens onto Arlington Street, she veered right, turning onto an intersecting walkway that led through a secluded wooded section before providing another egress at the far west end of the park onto the upper end of Beacon Street. The two men followed her into the treed area, with Bolan trailing behind.

In sharp contrast to the open grassy areas, the wooded quadrant occupying the northwest corner of the public gardens was deserted. Although the sun shone brightly, the lighting in the woods was significantly dimmer under a dark green canopy of centuries-old oaks that completely blocked the view of Boston's skyline.

Rodrigues continued leading them farther and farther into the wooded section, distancing them from other people. Bolan felt more comfortable tracking the trio in this environment, and although there were no tourists in sight once they got onto the dirt paths, every once in a while the aroma of marijuana reminded him that innocent bystanders were present, visible or not.

At a point roughly halfway through the woods to the exit onto Beacon Street, Rodrigues suddenly dodged onto a side path and broke into a full run. Her abrupt change in behavior caught her followers flat-footed, and they dashed forward to get her back in sight. Executing a response that surprised Bolan, they both reached into their jackets, withdrawing the same type of FN Five-seveN pistols the guards at the monastery in Bayonne had been carrying. As they assumed a firing stance, Bolan concluded that their instructions had to have been to prevent a meeting at all costs. Thinking that their prey was giving them an unrecoverable slip, they were jumping directly to the final solution.

"Stop!" Bolan shouted in a command voice reverberating with authority. "Drop the guns!"

They ignored his direction, instead diving in opposite directions while squeezing a few rounds down the path where the reporter had gone. Even without sound suppressors, the light pops of their 5.7 mm rounds were immediately swallowed by the broad oak leaves and dense vegetation. Bolan's

Beretta coughed once in response, the 9 mm round whizzing through the air where one of the followers had been an instant earlier, impacting into the thick trunk of an old oak where its entry hole emitted a thin tendril of white smoke. Realizing that they had lost their initial target, the gunmen turned their fire toward Bolan, who threw himself behind a two-foot-high outcropping breaking through the surface of a thick mossy carpet stretching between a few clumps of trees.

As 5.7 mm lead zeroed in on his position, sparking and whining in ricochets off the rocks affording him cover, Bolan considered his next move. Of primary importance was to keep them from going after Rodrigues. The way she had conducted herself impressed him, but even had she not, he didn't want the Order's thugs killing an innocent person.

Although she was not a major element in Bolan's overall plan, he was disturbed that the Order knew to follow her in the first place. No one outside of Stony Man Farm should have been aware that they were planning a meeting. He doubted he would be able to resolve the current situation with one of these gunmen still alive for him to interrogate, but the topic of a security leak was a question he'd return to until he found the answer.

Hoping he could correctly assess what someone with his enemies' limited combat training might do, Bolan thought they'd quickly realize they could achieve their objective to prevent a meeting by eliminating either party. If they were smart, they'd try to flank his position by alternatively covering each other while they advanced. The fact that they had not killed Rodrigues earlier when they had ample opportunity to do so indicated they were not one hundred percent sure of their intelligence or they were hoping she would lead them to him. If the Order somehow also knew that he was the one who attacked L'Abbaye de Raphael, their strategy to be patient—allowing her to make initial contact with the man who had left their facility at Bayonne in ruins—made sense. Logically, Bolan thought he should be their primary target.

As if the gunmen could read his thoughts, Bolan realized that the steady stream of lead cutting the air inches above his head was coming from one gunman. The other was obviously on the move. Pulling his legs under him like coiled springs, he waited for a break indicating that the covering gunman was changing magazines. When it finally came, he launched himself into a horizontal dive, searching for the flanking gunman during the seconds it took to fly through the air from the rocks to a position behind a pine sapling. Simultaneous with a landing that puffed an irritating cloud of pine needle dust into his face, he located his target moving in a crouch off to his left.

With his Beretta whispering potential death in single shots, Bolan fired and rolled away from the sapling to obtain more substantial cover behind an old elm whose gnarled roots had emerged from the soil and reentered so many times they looked like a nest of snakes at the base of the tree.

The covering gunman hosed Bolan's new location with a steady stream of automatic fire from his small pistol, but his angle wasn't exactly right, and the soldier was able to peer around the far side of his tree and see the advancing half of the duo as the man prepared to make a dash for a spot closer to Bolan's position. An instant before the gunman sprang forward, exposing himself for a two-second sprint, Bolan thumbed the Beretta's selector switch to 3-round burst. A leather loop sewn onto his shoulder holster held a

spare magazine loaded with twenty rounds of 9 mm Parabellum slugs, and although he had already expended five
from the clip in use, he thought firing in bursts would be
more effective in this setting. Against two foes he considered to be poorly trained due to the way they had been following Rodrigues, he didn't think he'd need more than his
remaining thirty-five rounds to bring this situation to a sat-
isfactory close.

The approaching gunman made his dash, and with 5.7 mm
lead from his partner snapping the air a few inches to the left
of Bolan's head, the soldier calmly squeezed a three-round
burst from his Beretta. The full metal-jacketed rounds caught
the man in midstride, stitching a diagonal pattern from shoulder to waist across the front of his torso. The combined force
of the three bullets tossed him into the woods as if he were
a rag doll. The attacker was dead before he hit the ground,
the only movement from his corpse being a steady flow of
blood from the wounds that rapidly spread across the front
of his warm-up jacket until they merged into one huge stain.

Directing his attention to the remaining gunman, Bolan
returned fire while scanning the area separating them,
searching for an attack lane. Ten yards to his right was one
of the rock walls that ran through the woods, constructed of
boulders roughly half the size of a man, thrown together
haphazardly as were most farmer's walls throughout New
England.

The wall was approximately waist high and as straight as
an arrow, leading directly behind the surviving gunman's
spot.

Bolan took a deep breath, mentally calculated the rounds
remaining in his magazine, and with a flurry of 3-round
bursts to keep his adversary in place, took two quick steps

before diving over the wall. He landed hard, banging his forehead on the irregular back side of one of the underlying rocks, the impact causing him to see stars for an instant.

From his new position, Bolan clearly held the upper hand. He knew his enemy was too far away to accurately gauge exactly where he was behind the rock barrier that could lead him directly behind the other man's position. Bolan, being pressed against the wall's opposite side, was able to put his face against the rocks and see through the cracks. As he inched closer to his adversary, the soldier heard the man's 5.7 mm rounds pinging against the other side of the wall in an attempt to draw him out. It was an amateur tactic, with no chance of success.

Apparently sensing that his current position was untenable, the remaining gunman lost the battle of patience and made an ill-advised move toward a spot ten feet farther into the woods. Bolan immediately rose, firing two tribursts in rapid succession.

The bullet that killed the gunman struck him in the upper cheek just below his ear, drilling a neat circle in the side of his face before exploding out the other side in a crimson spray. His head was jerked so fiercely to the side that his entire body turned as he began falling, in much the same way a diver's body follows the direction the head takes. Carried forward by his momentum, he took a few wobbly steps before his legs collapsed, crumbling him to the ground where he assumed an awkward position with legs twisted under his body.

In the distance, Bolan could hear the sounds of approaching sirens. They were coming fast, negating the opportunity for him to search his victims. With a final glance at the bloodied corpses, he slipped his Beretta into its holster and calmly walked away, following the same path Rodrigues had taken until it led him in less than a minute to the busy intersection of Arlington and Beacon Streets.

As he stepped onto the concrete sidewalk teeming with pedestrians who displayed a penchant for crossing dangerous city streets whenever and wherever they wished, Bolan could see the reflections of flashing blue lights a few blocks distant as police vehicles sped into the garden's entrance by the Washington statue.

"What's happening?" a woman's voice at his left elbow asked.

Bolan ignored the question and inched away, intent on melting into the crowd that due to the excitement generated by the showy arrival of police cars and vans, was growing larger by the second.

"Huh, Cooper?" the voice asked again. "What's happening in there?"

At the mention of the name, Bolan turned. Rodrigues was inches away, a determined look on her face. "There's a skywalk on top of the Prudential building," she said softly. "I'll meet you there in half an hour."

Bolan nodded and stole a glance at his watch. When he looked up a second later, the reporter had already disappeared into the crowd.

6

The Prudential Tower with its Skywalk Observation Deck was one of the tallest buildings in Boston. The city itself is relatively small, and from most locations anywhere in town, the top of the building the natives call The Pru, with its full name prominently displayed in block letters just below the roofline, can be seen. From the observation deck, people looking west could peer across Back Bay directly into Fenway Park, which on game nights stood out against the dark city like a fiery emerald.

Bolan threaded his way through the sidewalk crowd outside the public gardens to the T station at the corner of Boylston and Arlington streets where he could take the Green Line directly to the Prudential Tower. Boston's well-developed subway system with its routes on the Red, Green, Orange and Blue Lines was clearly marked.

The subway platform beneath Boylston Street where the outgoing train would depart for the Prudential building was sparsely populated with students using the T to cut across town to get up to Boston University, Red Sox fans opting to ride rather than walk the mile and a half from the gardens area to Copley Square, and tourists traveling to various attractions along the Green Line that included

Trinity Church, the Hancock Tower and Boston's public library.

A stringed quartet composed of young women dressed in identical long black dresses were playing Mozart from a spot close to the subway's entrance. A sign placed in an open violin case in front of the folding chairs and music stands the performers had arranged in a tight semicircle declared they were students from the Berklee College of Music a few blocks away. As he passed, Bolan dropped a few dollars into the open case, the contents of which were a woeful testament of public appreciation for the skill level the young musicians were displaying.

While waiting for the train, Bolan found his eyes zeroing in on the hands of everyone he saw, on alert for the presence of diamond scars. When he contacted Stony Man Farm, he'd ask Kurtzman's team to research the scar's significance. As with most secret cults, he suspected there was probably an initiation process into the Order of Raphael that for reasons known only to members, included disfiguring their left hand.

In the distance, a rumbling similar to approaching thunder echoed through the subway tunnel onto the loading platform. As the engine drew closer, the ground trembled, mimicking the tremors of a minor earthquake. The sound grew steadily louder, cresting to a deafening crescendo when the lead car burst from the tunnel. The airy screeching of hydraulic brakes added their voices to the din, bringing the speeding train to an abrupt halt.

The doors to a dozen cars stretching the entire length of the platform slid open, and Bolan chose the one he thought contained the fewest riders. The car was approximately half full, with a majority of passengers dressed in Red Sox attire of one type or another.

Bolan preferred to stand for the short three-stop ride to the Prudential building, and took a spot close to the door. The train lurched forward, and he reached up with his left hand to grasp the steady rail overhead, keeping his right hand free. The train accelerated quickly, causing everyone standing to lean and sway in order to counter the centrifugal forces the car's abrupt forward motion caused.

"Going to the game?" an old man sitting close to Bolan asked as the car negotiated a sharp curve.

"No. Just visiting," Bolan replied in a voice he hoped would convey his disinclination to carry on a conversation. He was more familiar to the etiquette expected on Washington's Metro, where passengers rode in silence, isolating themselves from their fellow commuters by burying their faces in newspapers, magazines and paperbacks. The propensity of T riders to strike up conversations with anyone within speaking distance struck him as oddly humorous.

"Where you from?" the old man persisted.

"D.C."

"Nationals, huh? Don't know why you guys didn't just reuse the name Senators. That's where your history is. *Damn Yankees,* and all. Ever see that musical?"

He looked up with rheumy eyes, searching Bolan's face for an answer.

"No," Bolan replied.

"Not a fan?"

"No." Bolan looked away, hoping his disinterest would stem the conversation.

The man turned in his seat to talk to the person next to him, who apparently was a baseball fan, because they immediately became engrossed in a conversation involving relief pitchers that drew unsolicited albeit passionate comments from a passenger across the aisle wearing a Red Sox cap that looked like it had been through a war.

The train reached the Copley stop, where roughly half the car emptied. In addition to being the exit for the public library, Copley was a good place to get off for access to the fashionable shops one block away on Newberry Street.

Glancing at the subway system's map on the wall near the door, Bolan was able to see that the Prudential building was the Green Line's next stop. It was closer than Copley had been to Arlington, and the train barely accelerated to a steady velocity before it began decelerating, its braking accompanied by the annoying screech of hydraulic air. The doors slid open, and Bolan stepped onto the platform against the tide of a handful of college students carrying beat-up musical cases that they bumped and scraped against the doorway and each other as they maneuvered them into place by open seats.

Upon disembarking, Bolan quickly walked the length of the loading platform, taking the stairs to street level two at a time. Outside on Huntington Avenue, tourists were climbing into two refurbished World War II amphibious assault vehicles painted to resemble cartoon ducks.

Bolan walked quickly up the wide concrete stairs to the Prudential lobby, bought a ticket to the observation deck, which came with a little silver lapel pin designating him a skywalker, and took the express elevator to the top lobby.

Stepping outside the gift shop that all elevator passengers had to walk through in order to get onto the open air observation deck, he was thankful that concealing his Beretta had forced him to wear a windbreaker. A cold salty wind gusting off the harbor howled intermittently at this elevation where it was at least ten degrees cooler than at street level.

Leslie Rodrigues was standing in the observation deck's northeast corner, looking out across the city below. As Bolan approached, a puff of wind ruffled her white miniskirt, exposing a generous flash of well-toned thigh.

Bolan sidled up next to her and rested his elbows on the ledge supporting the backward-sloping chain-link fence that prevented crazies from using the deck as a diving board into eternity.

"Did you kill them?" she asked without looking his way.

"You were very good," he said instead of answering her question. "How did you know you were being followed?"

"Patterns," she said with a shrug. "I'm good at recognizing all types of patterns. Those guys were really obvious."

Without wasting any time beating around the bush, Bolan said, "Two years ago, you wrote a series of articles about Australian scientists developing bioweapons."

"The superbug stories," she replied with a short nod and a faraway glance as if she was recalling the articles. "Scary stuff. Are you from Homeland Security?"

"What can you tell me about Terrance MacPherson? Was his team close to developing a pandemic level disease?"

She turned to look at him, and, with her face expressing her displeasure at being in the situation she currently found herself, said, "I'm usually the one asking the questions, Mr. Cooper. You're a man who comes out of nowhere, has no trace references in any of my research databases and sets up a meeting that places me directly in harm's way."

"Tell me about MacPherson," Bolan said.

She spoke rapidly, conveying a desire to end her contact with Bolan as soon as possible. "His team developed the process, publishing their work back in 1999, when terrorism was something that occasionally occurred in faraway places. Nevertheless, their report, *The New Terror,* along with an article in the *New Scientist* magazine about the team's pending report in the *Journal of Virology,* raised such alarm throughout the scientific community that they backed off, terminating the project. There's a semisecret organization called JASON you may want to contact. It's comprised of fifty or so independent scientists who advise the government about national security issues. Back in 1999, two years before 9/11, JASON scientists foresaw the emerging terrorist threat and regarded MacPherson's discoveries as developing the potential to create bioweapons that could be as devastating as nuclear devices."

"Their science was good?"

"It was good enough to scare the Australian government and a team of very dedicated scientists into abandoning a project they were convinced would save billions of dollars per year." Rodrigues nodded again, short and quick. "Yeah, their science was plenty good."

"How hard do you think it is to develop a bioweapon like what they were working on?" Bolan asked.

She shrugged and looked him in the face. When their eyes met, her expression softened and she sighed. "I've been away from that for more than two years. The scientists at JASON are the people you want to ask."

"Fair enough," Bolan answered. "I'm sorry we put you in danger. I hope this ends it for you."

"Me, too. Anything else you need?"

He hesitated for a moment, then said, "One last thing. Can we see a place called the Fens from here?"

"Other side," she said, motioning with her head. "Come on."

They walked around the observation deck's perimeter to

reach the west side, where Rodrigues pointed five or six blocks away to a sizeable wooded area with a narrow river running north to south through the center. Beyond the Fens, Bolan could see Fenway Park, home of the Boston Red Sox.

"Fen is an old English word for swampy land," Rodrigues said as Bolan studied the huge expanse where half a dozen Fenway Parks could easily fit. "The Fens were named in colonial times. Shortly thereafter, the road encircling them became the Fenway, and a century later the ballpark built a block away was named Fenway Park." She smiled and added, "Both the happiest and saddest place on earth."

She eyed him for a moment before displaying a level of intuition that sometimes marked the difference between a good and a great reporter by saying, "It's not a safe place at night. There's gang activity in there, and dumb people get mugged after dark."

"Is it patrolled by police?" Bolan asked.

"They tried for a while, but it's too big to control. It's also very isolated. Back in the sixties, organized crime gangs conducted full-scale gun battles in there without anyone even hearing them two blocks away. I'm telling you, the Fens is a dangerous place at night."

Bolan continued staring, and she added, "The name of that water you see running through the Fens is the Muddy River. It's an appropriate name. It would be hard for someone to cross by wading through."

"Does it empty into the Charles?"

"Yeah, it does. Through a culvert under Memorial Drive."

"Do you know how deep it is?"

Without glancing his way, she said, "Probably neck high for you in the middle," which told Bolan she had already made a number of assessments about him even before she added, "The culvert is long, maybe a quarter of a mile. It might be over your head in there, but the water never fills more than three-quarters of the way up. You could swim through it if you don't mind getting the weapon in your shoulder holster wet. I've gone the entire length both ways in a two-man scull."

7

Some cities, notably New York and Los Angeles, never sleep. Boston was not in that category. After taking a taxi from his hotel on the other side of Beacon Hill to the Hynes Auditorium next door to the Prudential building, Bolan walked five blocks on a route tracing a backward Z to the corner of Agassiz Road and Park Drive without once encountering another person. The sidewalk lighting was good, the grounds surrounding office buildings along Boylston and the Fenway were illuminated, and at no time during his quick hike did he feel threatened.

He was wearing black pants tucked into jump boots and a white polo shirt. Over his shoulder, where in less public environments devoid of policemen and taxicabs he would have been carrying his combat bag, he held a bright red Northeastern University backpack with an ease that belied the weight of the objects within.

Bolan had selected the corner of Agassiz and Park because that location allowed him to enter the Fens on the Park Drive side of the Muddy River where the Order of Raphael's facility was situated. In this portion of the city, a naturally occurring back bay extension to Boston Harbor had been filled in during colonial times and planted with thousands of trees to reclaim useable land from the ocean. The resulting woods reached south another half mile to the Metropolitan Museum of Fine Arts, but the section officially known as the Back Bay Fens was a quarter-mile square beginning at Agassiz and following Park Drive until running into the Massachusetts Turnpike at the small forest's northern boundary. It was along that northern perimeter that the Muddy River—which was more than thirty yards wide in most places—entered the culvert Rodrigues had told him about.

After taking a quick glance in all directions to ensure he was alone, Bolan stepped off the sidewalk and entered the Fens. Before he had progressed a dozen steps, he was pleased to note that the wooded section was significantly thicker than the one Rodrigues had led him and her followers into earlier that day in the corner of the public gardens across town. Bolan believed a battleground comprised of thick vegetation would afford him a competitive advantage in almost any situation.

In view of the fact that the Order had somehow learned he was in Boston, Bolan was not expecting to probe their building without meeting resistance. Knowing in advance there was an escape route through thick woods across the street from his objective provided a certain level of assurance to the warrior who had cut his combat teeth in jungles spanning the globe from Southeast Asia to Central America.

Once removed from the halo of streetlights, Bolan shrugged out of his backpack and emptied its contents onto the ground while his eyes began adjusting to the darkness. Assuming a kneeling position, he stripped off his white polo shirt, stuffed it into the backpack and donned a black, long-sleeved shirt with two front pockets, each reinforced to hold the weight of a fully loaded 20-round clip.

Bolan was not planning to carry ammo in his shirt pockets this night. In the backpack, he had brought his combat web belt with two pouches containing eighty .44-caliber bullets and four additional 20-round clips of 9 mm full-metal jacketed Parabellum rounds for the Beretta 93-R, which was cradled in a black leather holster under his left shoulder armpit. A third pouch, a bit longer and deeper than the ones designed to hold ammunition magazines, held his night-vision goggles and a mountaineering pistol with six pitons. A thin one hundred foot strand of high-tech composite carbon cable was looped in a neat figure eight on top of the pitons.

After slipping his arms through the belt's suspenders and buckling it at the waist, he stood to his full height and secured the holster holding the heavy Desert Eagle against his right hip. With his natural night vision reaching a level enabling him to see rough outlines, Bolan reached down and grabbed the weathered black cowhide sheath holding his razor-sharp Fairbairn-Sykes combat knife. After attaching the sheath to the outside of his left calf, he snatched the tube containing a three-color mixture of camouflage face paint and smeared an irregular pattern of green, brown and black swirls on the high points of his face.

While walking with silent steps across the carpet of decaying leaves and pine needles of the Fens, Bolan touch-checked his gear, tightening loose straps to ensure everything was snug. In order to practice the level of noise discipline required on a nighttime battlefield, a soldier had to make sure there was nothing loose enough to slap or rattle. Too many times to count, Bolan had zeroed in on an unseen enemy whose final mistake in life had been a failure to be neat, tight and tidy.

The night was cool, with a slight breeze gusting inland off Boston Harbor carrying a salty tang that refreshed Bolan's lungs as he sucked in the sea air. Comparable to the night in Bayonne, the crescent moon was partially hidden behind rows of low-lying clouds, peeking out every now and then to illuminate the landscape for a few moments in dim silvery light. Night insects communicated up and down a scale encompassing a few octaves, their buzzing codes intermittently underscored by the bass grumbling of bullfrogs belching out their oddly syncopated songs.

Dressed entirely in black, with his face dulled to absorb rather than reflect the meager moonlight, Bolan progressed through the woods invisibly, quickly reaching the edge of an open field he estimated marked the halfway spot between his entry point and final objective. At the edge of the coppice, he dropped to one knee to pause and make a final assessment of his position and goals. Off to his right, the Muddy River formed a slight bend before heading straight north through the Fens on its way to the culvert emptying into the Charles, its surface shimmering metallic black in the cloud-filtered moonlight. Along its banks were clumps of bulrushes and ornamental swamp grasses growing tall enough to conceal a person. While the vegetation would provide excellent concealment, the flimsy foliage could do nothing to afford cover from even the smallest caliber weapons.

With his mind set relative to where he was and where he was going, Bolan pulled the night-vision goggles from their pouch and slipped them over his eyes. In the bright green landscape, the only movement the soldier saw on the field directly ahead was that of half a dozen jack rabbits cavorting in seemingly random patterns, zigzagging away from one another between quick encounters of doing what rabbits do on romantic moonlit nights.

Bolan knew wearing the goggles for an extended period of time significantly degraded the user's unassisted night vision. As soon as he verified that the field in front of him was empty, he removed the goggles, placed them back in their pouch and walked into the open area, moving at a swift pace to reach a thick stand of trees on the opposite side.

When he was approximately ten yards away, there was a sudden rustling in the bushes bordering the edge of the field, and a group of youths emerged to stand in a straight line before him.

Bolan recalled the warning about gangs and muggings in the Fens after dark, and realized he had walked into one of their ambushes. This gang apparently waited silently on the edge of the open field where the silhouette of a potential victim would stand out as a darker mass against the sky. It was a good tactic, one Bolan himself had successfully used on a number of occasions while staking ambushes.

Remaining calm, as if being confronted by a gang of punks was an every day occurrence, Bolan took swift inventory of the youths and their weapons. There were eight, a number he was comfortable taking on, and except for three who held short aluminum baseball bats, the group appeared to be unarmed. All wore thin silver chains attached to their pants in a loop from their belt to knee-high side pockets, the metal sparkling dully in the dim light.

An instant before he snatched the Desert Eagle from its holster to scare them into leaving him alone so he could continue his mission, the distinctive click of a Glock's safety being turned off told Bolan his initial assessment, hampered by the darkness, had been incorrect. The youth second to the right of the one in the center held a .40-caliber pistol.

"Hey, motherfucker," one of them said, sneering, "you need to pay a toll to go through here."

"My business is not your business," he replied calmly. "Let me pass."

"You deaf, man? No one goes through here without paying."

In unison so precise it gave the appearance they were connected by a rod running through their hips, the entire eight took a few steps forward while one of the youths switched on a flashlight. Bolan immediately closed his right eye to keep from losing all his night vision. He realized that once the light was out, he'd have an advantage over the gang members whose eyes would take a few minutes to readjust, but his preference remained to get away from them as fast as possible to complete his intended mission.

With the beam from the flashlight playing over Bolan's camouflaged face, web belt, and pistols, the youth with the Glock stepped forward, holding the weapon straight out in front of him with both hands.

"Whoa!" he exclaimed from about ten feet away. "We got ourselves a fuckin' GI Joe here."

"All you've got is the point man for a squad that can take you down," Bolan said with such authority that two of the boys near the line's left end began nervously looking beyond him to the woods from where he had emerged. All of a sudden, Bolan emitted a shrill whistle that cut sharply through the night air. "Now," he said while motioning with his head to the kid holding the pistol, "if he fires that Glock, you'll all die tonight. And get that light off of me! Now!"

The flashlight was abruptly switched off, and Bolan

opened his other eye. His depth perception had suffered, but not to the extent that he couldn't see the boy with the Glock start to lower the pistol until it was by his side. Then for reasons known only to him, he changed his mind and quickly began raising it.

Bolan had seen the exact sequence too many times to doubt the outcome, and he abruptly threw himself to the side, diving horizontally through the air to his left while drawing the Desert Eagle with his right hand. A millisecond after the Glock's .40-caliber round sliced through the air where he had been, Bolan's Desert Eagle roared in response, its retort incredibly loud against the stillness of the Fens. The hefty .44-caliber slug smashed the Glock into a piece of useless steel while removing most of the gangbanger's hand in the process. He howled in anguish and fell back, unconscious from the excruciating pain before he was halfway to the ground.

Bolan rolled immediately upon hitting the dirt, assuming a prone position three yards back and to the left, with his legs coiled beneath him, ready to launch his body in a different direction. The flashlight came back on for less than a second before Bolan expressed his displeasure with a round that hit the youth holding the light in the wrist, spinning him clockwise while the flashlight and a healthy helping of flesh flew to the rear.

"Do you all want to die?" Bolan shouted.

"No! Don't shoot!" came from a number of mouths, all expressing the same message, some utilizing a variety of words.

"Get them out of here!" Bolan commanded, raising to a crouch and moving silently to the left so he could sprint and get behind them.

There was a flurry of activity as the unharmed gang members rushed to the aid of their fallen comrades. While they were engaged in picking up their wounded comrades who moaned and cursed furiously, Bolan flanked the line to the left and dashed for the trees ten yards beyond, rushing a few steps into the woods as his left eye's night vision rapidly recovered, improving his depth perception by the second. When he was roughly ten yards beyond the field's edge, he found a spot behind a thick oak, settled himself into a kneeling position against the protective trunk and pulled his night-vision goggles from their pouch.

In the greenish glow, he could see the youths dragging their injured members down a dirt path he knew would exit the Fens onto Park Drive. Wounding two punks who never had a chance against someone with Bolan's skills was unfortunate not only because it delayed his mission, but also because he regretted engaging in avoidable violence against young people, despite their criminal behavior. He fully understood he had just maimed two young men perhaps for life, but he also knew the outcome of their confrontation could have been worse. If they had been foolish enough to attempt disarming him, he could have ended up killing them all.

While he waited for the gang members to clear the immediate area, Bolan ejected the magazine from his Desert Eagle, placing it into the ammo pouch where he retrieved a fresh one that he slipped into the ammo port. Although he had expended only two cartridges during his brief encounter with the gang, Bolan wanted to reach his objective with a full load ready to rock and roll if the need arose. After waiting a few minutes while he thought of the possible scenarios he'd shortly face, he hitched his web belt into place by tugging lightly on the suspenders, rose, and resumed his approach.

The Order of Raphael's building was a three-story brick structure nestled between two skyscrapers—one housing an insurance company, the other a software firm—on a quiet section of Park Drive three blocks south of where it merged with Boylston Street. Lush, perfectly flat strips of lawn ten-feet wide ran down both sides of the building. Were it not for the attractive plantings and occasional trees placed symmetrically from front to back, the facility would have appeared to be bordered on each side by well-tended bocce courts.

Rather than attempt a frontal assault, Bolan decided to approach from the rear, where he'd be beyond the glow from Park Drive's sidewalk streetlamps. Remaining under the concealing umbrella of the Fens' foliage, he walked a few hundred yards beyond the building before crossing the deserted thoroughfare and doubling back. When he reached the back corner of the software company's property, he slipped the night-vision goggles over his eyes, switching the unit to infrared mode.

As he painted his objective with IR, the landscape before him shimmered slightly while the goggle's internal cathode tubes adjusted to a new data stream. Once they began processing real time, Bolan saw the implications of the Order knowing he was coming. There were IR security nets everywhere.

Appearing crisp and red behind the lenses, laser-thin beams crossed in a tight grid designed with overlay redundancy along the ground and up the side of the building to the second floor. The lawn between buildings was a minefield of IR sensors, positioned to ensure that no one could get anywhere close to the building without alerting security personnel inside. All window openings on the first two floors had been bricked over, apparently at some point in the past, but from his spot next door, Bolan could see moonlight reflecting off the third floor panes of glass roughly forty feet above ground level. If he was to enter the facility, it would have to be through one of the third-floor windows.

Moving in a low crouch allowing him to be almost invisible against the dark background, Bolan took care to stay off the grassy strip while he moved along the side of the software firm until he reached a point next to one of the trees. The outer facade of the high-tech company's building was composed of concrete and glass, with wide strips of concrete up and down, front and back, giving the structure the appearance of a giant checkerboard placed on its side. Slabs of concrete separating the glass squares were roughly four feet wide, perfect for the plan forming in Bolan's mind.

He removed his goggles and put them into the pouch containing his mountaineering pistol and the pitons. CIA scientists had treated the sharp end of the pitons with their version of a superglue that was activated by the instantaneous friction resulting from the tip of the piton piercing an extremely tiny hole in wood, concrete and all but the hardest of stones. After the glue had been demonstrated to Aaron Kurtzman in one of the labs at Stony Man Farm, he told Barbara Price the presentation reminded him of a magician's trick the way they fired a narrow pin less than a millimeter into the side of a concrete slab, waited ten seconds, then hung five one hundred pound weights onto the pin that appeared to be barely touching the slab.

Bolan threaded the thin strand of high-tech cable into a double back loop through two of his pitons, took careful aim with the pistol and fired the first spike into a concrete cross-beam approximately forty feet above his head. After waiting ten seconds, he pulled hard on the cable, leaning back on his heels to make sure the tip was set. Once he was sure it would support his weight, he repeated the process with a second piton shot into the same concrete slab five or six feet from the first.

Tugging the cable taut to remove unwanted slack, he formed a long skinny triangle with the pitons sticking into the wall forty feet off the ground forming two of the triangle's points with him being the third. By alternately pulling with opposite arms, first on the right then on the left cable, Bolan was able to walk up the side of the building, shrinking the area within the triangle as he brought the angle he represented closer to the other two. When he was roughly thirty feet high, he grasped both lines in his left hand and leaned away from the building, causing the tendons in his forearm to bulge under the stress. Setting himself at a forty-five-degree angle to the glass-and-concrete structure, he aimed the pistol at a spot above his head on the maple tree growing between him and the Order's brick building. With his gun hand held perfectly still, he fired a piton trailing a length of cable threaded and tied with a tight square knot into the center of the tree's trunk.

The metal spike struck home with a resounding *thunk* that told Bolan the point had penetrated deeper into the wood than the two currently supporting his weight. He secured the cable onto the piton closest to him with another square knot so it wouldn't slip through the eye as it had done when he used double back loops to scale the building. With the line connecting the close piton to the one in the tree pulled as straight as a tightrope, he held his body in place with his right hand while he put the mountaineering pistol away before reaching with his left to the scabbard on his calf. His combat knife easily sliced through the cable looped through the pitons he had used to climb the software company's wall, and he reeled in the freed segment for use once he got to the maple.

Utilizing the same technique he had employed with combat teams to ford rivers, he locked his ankles over the cable, suspending himself upside down like a sloth on a vine in the rain forest. By using a hand-over-hand motion, he quickly slid himself from the outside wall of the software firm's building into the branches of the tree standing less than twenty yards from the Order of Raphael's facility.

Not unexpectedly, Bolan found firing the mountaineering pistol while standing on a sturdy branch thirty-five feet off the ground to be considerably easier than making his previous shot into the tree while hanging in midair off the side of a building. A piton trailing the length of cable he had cut with his combat knife flew straight as an arrow into the brick wall, embedding itself inches from where he was aiming. Using the same hand-over-hand technique that had transported him to the tree, he traversed the distance between the tree and building, bringing himself to a position on an ornate ledge outside one of the third-floor windows.

Donning his night-vision goggles, Bolan peered into the darkness beyond the glass. The room he was outside of appeared to be an office. There were file cabinets against the length of one side wall, two large worktables pushed together in the middle of the room on which dozens of manila folders were stacked in neat piles, and six ergonomic desk chairs placed around the tables. A white grease board with sections written in blue, red and green markers covered the entire opposite wall. Most importantly, there did not seem to be infrared beams on either the inner or outer surface of the window.

As he was reaching into his web belt for a diamond-tipped glass cutter and suction cup, the soft sounds of conversation below caught his attention. Two men dressed in the same type of running suits as those worn by the duo following Rodrigues into the public gardens were walking beneath his spot, speaking softly. Through the lenses of his goggles, Bolan could see they were maintaining a wide berth from the IR security beams running along the side of the building at ground level. A replay of the first two guards he encountered outside the walls at L'Abbaye de Raphael flashed through his brain.

In ultra-slow motion, Bolan reached into his shoulder holster, withdrew the Beretta 93-R and thumbed the fire selector to 3-round bursts. There was a very good chance these two would pass by without looking up, but the soldier had not survived his countless years on battlefields by trusting the odds even in those instances when they were overwhelmingly in his favor. More times than he cared to remember, he had heard a medic in the field refer to one of his comrades as a "one in a million chance" while attaching a KIA tag before zipping the body bag closed. In the hellish environment called combat, it often seemed that the unlikely happened all the time—the unthinkable became commonplace.

Bolan listened hard to the cadence of the conversation. When they paused for a moment and switched to French while slowly slipping their hands into the front of their running jackets, he knew he had been detected. Without waiting to make sure, he cut loose with the Beretta before the guards could withdraw their weapons.

The 93-R's first 3-round burst hit the man on the right in the top of his head, hammering him to the ground four feet distant. He landed on his back, arms flayed to the sides in a bed of blooming geraniums.

His partner was struck less than a second later by a tri-burst of 9 mm Parabellum lead that caught him in the upper chest below his chin. The downward angle of fire drove the bullets through his heart from the top left ventricle, exiting through his right buttock. In a final spasm of nervous energy, he staggered two steps forward, arms windmilling, before crashing face-first directly onto the infrared beams forming a security net at the building's base. Pandemonium erupted inside as alarm bells and sirens suddenly proclaimed that an intruder was on the premises.

Moving his hands with eye-blurring speed, Bolan ripped off his night-vision goggles, shoved them into their pouch and drew his combat knife from its calf sheath. Grabbing the cord connected to the maple tree twenty yards away, he sliced it free and launched himself away from the building into a Tarzan-type swing. His hold slipped when he was still too high to let go, and he squeezed tighter, clenching the cord with both hands as he swung toward the ground.

The bottom of the pendulous arc brought Bolan to within ten feet of the ground, where he released his grip, sailing through the air for a few seconds before hitting the manicured lawn hard. He scrambled to regain his feet, battling the momentum that propelled him forward, and dashed directly across the sidewalk onto Park Drive.

Halfway across the road to the relative safety of the Fens, he came under fire from automatic weapons, their chilling chatter filling the night air. He lowered his head while zig-zagging back and forth, all the time willing his feet to go

faster. When he was close enough to dive over the far sidewalk into the dense vegetation lining the Fens, he did so, accompanied by lead flying a finger's width above his head.
All about him, bullets buzzed, one grazing the surface of his
cheek a microsecond before he hit the ground.

Without the slightest indication of conscious direction,
his hands found their instruments of death, and Bolan came
out of a somersault landing on the other side of Park Drive
with both guns blazing.

Half a dozen guards were in hot pursuit, hosing the area
in his vicinity with a steady stream of 5.7 mm rounds. He
rolled to the right, firing the Desert Eagle as quickly as he
could pull the trigger, the first two of the pistol's hefty slugs
catching the leading guard in his gut. He crashed into the
middle lane of Park Drive, bouncing a few times before his
corpse came to its final rest.

Quickly shifting his aim, Bolan fired the Desert Eagle
twice in such rapid succession the retort echoed through the
Fens as if it was a single shot. Both rounds hit the same gunman, stopping his advance cold. He leaned back as if his feet
had been nailed to the street, his finger frozen in a death grip
on the trigger of the submachine gun he carried. Rounds
traced a half circle extending from inches above Bolan's
head to straight up into the sky before his magazine was
spent and the weapon lay as lifeless as its owner on the Boston street.

Bolan's other pursuers dived for the ground, firing as
best they could after landing hard on the asphalt's unyield-
ing surface. In return, Bolan fired his handguns as rapidly
as possible, keeping them down. When the Desert Eagle's
bolt clicked open on an empty chamber, he ejected the exhausted magazine, grabbed a fresh one from his ammo

pouch with the hand holding his Beretta, and rammed the
new clip home with the fluidity and precision of a ballet
move.

After letting loose with a combined barrage of full metal-
jacketed rounds from both his Desert Eagle and the Beretta,
Bolan turned and sprinted deeper into the Fens, seeking the
safety of the thick forest.

A few seconds elapsed before the Order of Raphael's
gunmen realized they were no longer pinned down, and
they jumped to their feet to follow his retreat. Bolan heard
them coming as they called out to one another and crashed
through the woods, but regardless of how inexperienced
they were in combat, they held a vast superiority of numbers and they were armed with submachine guns set to full-
auto. The combination did not bode well for the Executioner.

He spotted a pile of rocks a few yards away, and took up
position behind the cover they offered. A delaying stand
could dwindle their forces, enabling him to perhaps open an
escape lane if he could thin their ranks sufficiently.

When they came into the Fens, two began firing in the
direction they thought Bolan had taken, apparently hoping
to hit him by covering a wide-sweeping area with a wall of
lead. The tactic might have worked had they been in an
open field, but from his covered position behind the pile of
rocks, Bolan was able to zero in on the muzzle-flashes of
the gunmen. With single shots booming from his Desert
Eagle, he dropped the first two men who entered the forest.
Accompanied by a medley of angry cries, the four or five
gunmen on the heels of the lead men learned a critical firefight lesson and took immediate cover behind the trunks of
trees, firing from spots close to the ground. By the time the
lifeblood had drained from the two lead gunmen, their com-

patriots had all assumed positions of safety while they searched for the invader's location.

Crouched behind the cover of the rock pile, Bolan calculated his store of ammo. He still had more than sixty rounds for the Beretta, and a clip and a half of .44 slugs for the Desert Eagle, which would give him enough firepower to conduct an orderly retreat. Without the Order knowing how he planned to cross the Fens, there was no way they could follow him as he moved across the expansive wooded area. He'd remain engaged for a few more minutes to further reduce their membership, then beat feet out of the battle zone and live to fight another day. With their prey concealed behind the cloak of darkness, the Order's inexperienced soldiers would have no idea how to follow his trail.

Before peeking out from behind the rocks, Bolan slipped on his night goggles, switching them from infrared to ambient mode. About fifty yards away, two men were moving stealthily through the woods. From his position behind the rock, Bolan could see they were both wearing night goggles. This was his first evidence that the Order of Raphael had embraced night-vision technology, but given their sophisticated laboratories, their use of infrared security nets, and their choice of weapons with Kevlar-piercing capability, Bolan was not surprised to find night-vision goggles in their combat arsenal.

Leaning his chest against the rock pile so his head and shoulders were above the obstruction and thus able to get a clean line of fire, he holstered the Desert Eagle and lowered the Beretta's folding fore grip, transforming his handgun into a weapon with the feel resembling a mini-Uzi. With the added stability of the fore grip and the rock foundation to lean his torso and arms against, he checked the fire selector, making sure it was set for 3-round bursts. Of the half dozen men Bolan had counted pursuing him while out on the road, only two wore night-vision goggles. Since none of the others were armed with unique weapons to cause him undue concern, the enemies with night vision jumped to the top of the combat veteran's priority list.

The two were moving together as a team, appearing to help each other thread their way through the trees, their trepidation indicating that the use of night goggles was new to the Order. As they flitted from one tree to another, their heads sweeping from left to right searching for their target in what had to have been a slightly confusing landscape, Bolan remained perfectly still.

In the night-enhanced eye of an inexperienced user, as long as Bolan didn't move, he would be seen as nothing more than an irregular bump on top of a pile of rocks. As in daylight, it was motion that most often betrayed a soldier's position.

The pair with goggles were working physically close together, a mortal sin on the field of combat where a separation of five yards from your closest buddy was the minimum rule of thumb to ensure that one grenade or booby trap could not take out an entire squad. Their carelessness reinforced Bolan's opinion that actual combat was a recent activity for the Order of Raphael. The cult's members may have survived for centuries as spies, planners of evil, and surreptitious couriers of death—if the legend Barbara Price told the cybernetics team at Stony Man Farm group was to be believed—but life-or-death combat against a trained enemy, regardless of the quality of modern weapons they sported, appeared to be a new game for them.

As quickly as the opinion formed, a small voice in the

back of Bolan's mind warned him not to underestimate a clearly inferior enemy. Arrogance was another trait that more often than not invited death on the field of battle.

The duo with goggles finally rewarded Bolan's unflinching patience by attempting to sneak across a space roughly fifteen feet wide between two trees each with trunks broad enough that it would take three people linking hands to reach around their circumferences. When the attackers were perfectly framed, as if they were a photograph centered with an equal span of white space on both sides, Bolan let loose with three bursts from the Beretta.

It was difficult to tell how many of the nine steel-jacketed slugs hit each of the two gunners with night vision, so violently did their bodies twist and turn as the three 9 mm bursts found their marks. Each was hit multiple times.

The two wearing night goggles were no longer a threat. The first was hammered clean off his feet while being thrown a few yards off the trail, the soles of his shoes being the last thing he pointed at Bolan. His partner danced wildly for a few seconds under the lingering shock from the penetrating rounds before shimmying to the ground in an almost comical Elvis impersonation.

Their comrades, however, did not require the use of night goggles to immediately zero in on Bolan's position. They began hosing the surrounding area with a lethal barrage of 5.7 mm slugs as the racket of automatic fire echoed through the trees. Bullets striking the rocks in front of Bolan sent flinty splinters sparking and flying in all directions, filling the air with the ear-screeching whine of ricochets.

Pulling the goggles from his eyes and shoving them back into his pouch, Bolan used his enemies' muzzle-flashes as targets. There were four aggressors remaining, working in two teams armed with submachine guns chattering on full-auto. Dispensing a hail of lead from both hands, with the Desert Eagle's deep-throated voice announcing by nanoseconds its hefty slug's arrival, Bolan concentrated on the team to his left attempting a flanking movement.

Thinking they would expect him to continue his retreat deeper into the woods toward the Muddy River, Bolan loosed a torrent of well-aimed rounds from both weapons simultaneously, emptying the magazines in a thunderous volley sounding like the final display of a fireworks show on the Fourth of July. After ejecting the spent clips and ramming fresh ones into the ammo ports, he sprinted in a crouch to the cover of a small clump of birches, moving at an angle he calculated would intersect with the flanking team's path.

He continued an irregular pattern of dashing forward to find cover, followed immediately by a sideways traverse, thus navigating a course similar to that of a sailor tacking his craft against the wind. As he moved, he noted that both teams maintained their fire on the pile of rocks from where his last volley had come. Although a lack of response from the rocks grew long, his enemies continued tearing up clods of earth all around the obstruction, apparently believing their adversary was pinned down, or perhaps already dead. In either case, Bolan decided he would maintain strict fire discipline, remaining silent until he intersected the flanking pair.

He heard them before they became visible. Even without his goggles, Bolan's night vision had reached its natural peak, and he was easily able to discern the denser mass of a person's body moving across a vegetative background. To his left there was a thin stand of chestnut trees. Bolan assumed a kneeling position behind them, leaning into a hardwood trunk for support and stability.

He engaged the two attackers with his Desert Eagle when they were approximately twenty feet away. Firing two shots closely, he quickly eliminated the flanking pair.

The lead man caught the first delivery full in the chest, the beefy hunk of lead shattering his rib cage and organs within while lifting him completely off his feet before exiting through his back. The man crashed to the ground where his fingers twitched uncontrollably for a few moments despite the fact he had been dead an instant after the gunshot sounded, seconds before his body impacted the ground.

His partner, following a few feet behind, was drilled in the gut, which doubled him over as if he was bowing low for his final curtain call before exiting stage left into eternity. He, too, was shoved violently off the path by the force of the Desert Eagle's output, landing two or three yards into the low-lying wild blueberry bushes scattered throughout the Fens. He fell faceup, exposing a gaping wound oozing a copious amount of intestines below his belt.

Two left, Bolan thought as he turned away from the tattered corpses and began forming in his mind the approach he would use to hunt down the remaining pair. Before he had taken half a dozen steps in their direction, however, he heard the dogs.

The game had changed drastically. Bolan reversed direction, running as fast as he could to reach the open field where the Muddy River flowed. Until that moment, his superior expertise with weapons had put him on an even keel against a numerically superior force wielding automatic submachine guns. His years of experience using night-vision goggles had easily countered his enemies' threat when they attempted to adopt the same technology. His combat savvy, honed to a fine edge, had clearly afforded him a competitive advantage from the moment he lured his foes away from the open spaces on Park Drive into the thick foliage of the Fens.

Dogs were an entirely different matter. Trained hunters, leading a team of pursuers armed with automatic rifles, did not bode well for a solitary soldier retreating through a wooded area. As he ran at top speed across the open field with the thirty-foot-wide ribbon of water appearing in the distance as a strip of tranquil silver, he rummaged through his web belt for his night-vision goggles. The back strap was actually a thin tube of rubber designed to stretch and conform to the size of the user's head, ensuring that the lenses with their rubber eyecups were pulled snugly against the eye sockets. Without breaking stride, Bolan ripped the ten-inch section of tube from the back of the goggles before shoving them back into their pouch.

When he reached the Muddy River, which he planned to follow north to the culvert emptying into the Charles, he angled south for a few yards in order to enter the water. He thrashed through a clump of Asian ornamental grass growing on the banks where he could leave his scent for the dogs. As he wiped his face and hands on the thick wide blades, his ears calculated the dog team's progress. They were coming fast, eager in the hunt. Hoping that the reporter's assessment of the depth in the middle had been accurate, he plodded toward the river's center, learning firsthand why she had said its name was apt. The river's bottom was composed of soft sticky mud that seized and sucked his boots at every step as if demons below the surface were grasping his feet in an attempt to hold him in place.

Struggling to reach the center, he pulled his legs forward one step at a time, with the howling drawing closer by the second. He reached the middle of the river when he esti-mated the dogs were at the far end of the field. He immedi-ately headed north, hoping his pursuers would assume his entry trajectory through the grasses defined the direction in which he was escaping. If they started searching the area and found his backpack, they'd probably believe he was going south through the river, to exit the Fens the way he came in.

Once he reached the middle, Bolan found the muck underfoot was a bit less clinging, but walking north, even with the help of a minor current, was not easy. As the dogs drew close, the soldier stuck the rubber tube from the back of his goggles into his mouth and bent his knees slightly to submerge himself a few inches below the surface. He had trained for situations such as this, and experienced no prob-lem breathing entirely through his mouth. As he made his way slowly but steadily toward the escape culvert he esti-mated to be approximately two hundred yards to the north, not one drop of the murky water made its way up his nos-trils.

The dogs reached the river, the bloodcurdling sound of their barking muted by Bolan's head being under water, but not to an extent that prevented him from getting a good bearing on their position. As he had hoped, they were con-centrating on the tall grasses and swamp weeds growing along the banks a good ten or fifteen yards upstream from his current progress. When the humans arrived on the scene and realized the dogs had lost the scent, they sprayed the grasses and a section of water surrounding them with auto-matic fire. The staccato bursts sounded more and more dis-tant as Bolan continued his movement north, the only sign of his presence a thin rubber tube extending inches above the water's surface.

Bolan knew his pursuers had two choices—they too could wade through the water with their dogs and try to pick up a scent on the other side, or they could run the entire length of the river to the corner of Agassiz Road and Park Drive where he had entered the Fens, and attempt to find him from there. Neither choice was viable, but Bolan thought they might post a guard close to where he had left his backpack. Escaping through the culvert Rodrigues said emptied into the Charles was unquestionably his best option.

The murky water stung his eyes as he trudged north, leaving the barking dogs and his angry enemies farther and farther behind. It was pitch black under the water, so he kept his eyes closed for long periods of time, concentrating merely on keeping his entire body submerged without allowing the short tube to be pulled under the surface.

As he closed his mind to everything but the task at hand, he knew his escape at this point was a given, requiring nothing more than discipline and patience. His weapons would need a good cleaning and oiling once he got back to the hotel, but as far as eluding his pursuers was concerned, he could remain underwater in this manner for as long as it took.

WHEN HE RAISED HIS HEAD above the surface of the water to check for the culvert's opening, the Executioner saw it was less than four feet away. The Fens behind him were silent, and he knew his enemies had long since abandoned their pursuit.

With a gentle push off the muddy bottom, he began swimming, utilizing a silent breaststroke that propelled him through the concrete culvert's opening.

The current picked up once inside the defined space of

the drain, speeding him along on his quarter-mile swim to the Charles. When he was approximately halfway to the end opening, which appeared in the distance as a circle of less dense black, he realized he was swimming through a large pack of river rats. The rodents bumped against his face and arms, and he concentrated on gently pushing them away, moving smoothly and slowly, knowing they posed no harm to him unless he panicked them into thinking he was a menace. The rats sidled up against Bolan with no ill intent, swimming along on the current as if he were nothing more than a piece of driftwood.

When the culvert finally dumped them all into the greater expanse of the Charles River, Bolan swam a few hundred yards downstream to a boathouse used by the MIT crew team before he pulled himself out of the water and onto the cracked and weathered dock.

The lock securing the boathouse door was easy to pick, and inside Bolan found an old canvas duffel bag large enough to tote his gear so he wouldn't have to walk across town carrying his weapons in plain sight. There was a bathroom, and Bolan went in to wash his face in the sink. After using a paper towel to wipe away traces of camouflage paint not washed off in the Muddy River, he hefted the duffel bag over his shoulder and began a forty-five-minute walk to his hotel on the other side of Beacon Hill.

False dawn was painting the sky over the Expressway, producing the first wispy tendrils of pink clouds overhead when he finally reached the hotel, stinking and exhausted. He entered through a back kitchen entrance and took the service elevator to his floor. After a vigorous shower, Bolan fell into a restless sleep.

His last conscious thoughts questioned how the Order of

Raphael knew in advance that he was coming to Boston to meet with Leslie Rodrigues.

The answer, he hoped, would be forthcoming from Aaron Kurtzman and his team at Stony Man Farm.

8

"Missing?" Aaron Kurtzman echoed Barbara Price's words with a tone of skepticism, conveying his disbelief that the scientist's absence was anything other than a kidnapping by the Order of Raphael. He gazed around the conference table in the Stony Man Farm's War Room, receiving visual acknowledgment that his point was understood by Brognola and Bolan as well as the three members of his cybernetics team.

"Missing," the Farm's mission controller repeated. "One of our men checked out MacPherson's apartment," Barbara continued her briefing with a quick glance at her notes, "and then talked to dozens of neighbors in his building. MacPherson lives alone. No family, his wife died of breast cancer ten years ago. Immersing himself totally in his research is all he's done since. Comes and goes at odd hours, but nobody's seen him for weeks."

"None of the neighbors thought his absence was strange?" Wethers asked.

"Apparently he's a pleasant but somewhat reclusive man. Most residents in the apartment complex know he's a famous virologist, so they leave him alone to pursue his work. As far as our man could tell, no one has talked with or seen him for a while."

"The reporter in Boston told me he belongs to an organization called JASON," Bolan said, "a group of international scientists who advise the NSA on security matters. MacPherson may not talk much to his neighbors, but I'll bet he stays in touch with his professional colleagues. Especially if they're conducting cutting-edge research."

"We know about that group," Brognola said. "That's why we'd like you to go to Sydney, Striker. To meet with another researcher named Richard Hannigan, who was MacPherson's deputy on the mouse pox project that may have led to his current situation." He paused for a second. "We also want you to visit the Order's facility there. If MacPherson is being forced to work on the project the way Zagorski was in Bayonne, he could still be on-site. You may be able to pull off another snatch and rescue."

"Weapons?"

"I'll give you a contact in country," Brognola said.

"LaFontaine is the name of our contact in Sydney," Price interjected. "I'll tell him you're coming."

"They were expecting me in Boston," Bolan said to Brognola. "They won't be caught by surprise again."

"We have to pull that thread," the big Fed said while finger combing his hair. The seriousness of his tone conveyed his concern, making the others recall the last time there had been a leak involving Stony Man Farm. "No one should have known. It must have originated from the *Tribune*'s end."

Wethers shook his head slowly. "Newspaper reporter? I don't think so. They're better than most at keeping secrets."

"I'll find the leak," Brognola stated, allowing the team to move on to the planned topic for the meeting.

Kurtzman sipped a mouthful of coffee from a mug whose

interior was indelibly stained a deep chestnut brown from the special blend he created. Delahunt once remarked that it was a good thing the Stony Man Farm's cybernetics team had cast iron stomachs, as in her opinion, Aaron's coffee would undoubtedly cause ulcers.

After swallowing the potent brew, he said, "Sonia Zagorski told us the team at Bayonne was close to finishing their third of the project. I have two questions. Why would an organization attempting to create a bioweapon do it in three separate places? And, should we assume that the progress of the other two teams was roughly that of Dr. Zagorski's?"

"I can answer the first one," Wethers said. "I've done some independent research of my own and learned that with critically contagious substances, medical facilities often segregate the operational components, bringing them together in tightly controlled conditions only when the characteristics and stability of each element has been independently confirmed. A separation spanning continents is certainly not the rule, but the segregation itself reflects a disciplined approach."

"Probability is all three teams were equal," Tokaido said, his head swaying to the strains of music blasting through his ear buds. He snapped his bubble gum and added, "Striker only *delayed* the French team. They'll have records of what Zagorski did. Someone will pick up where she left off."

"But they no longer have her talent," Brognola said. "Her rescue must have been a serious blow to them."

"Delay," Tokaido repeated, the pink wad moving from one side of his mouth to the other as if the sugary substance possessed a life of its own.

Delahunt said, "I agree with Akira. It makes sense that the work would be divided so that one team would not finish too far behind the other two. The teams were probably pretty much equal in talent, and the work would have been divided accordingly. If Zagorski thought her team was close, I'll bet they all are. The team that finishes first will reconstruct her work and complete the French portion."

The room fell silent as those at the table considered the implications of a disease capable of ravaging the population of a continent the way the Black Death had devastated Europe.

"Worst case," Brognola asked, "how would they deploy it?"

"Countless methods," Delahunt replied, pressing her fingers against her temples to massage the stress she suddenly felt. "They could dump a virus into the drinking reservoirs for major cities, airborne viruses could be dispersed with crop dusters flying over metropolitan areas, they could release it into a subway system the way those terrorists did a few years ago in Japan. In a free society, the possibilities are endless. And then once it's released…" Her voice tapered off.

"I say they'll use the Forty Martyrs," Price stated, and all eyes turned to her. "I've continued to read everything I can find on this group."

Looking at Bolan, she said, "You asked about the diamond scars on the backs of their left hands. This organization is steeped in history. Everything they do is ritualistic. Members undergo an initiation ceremony during which a spike, believed to be similar to the ones the Romans used to nail Jesus to the cross, is driven through the soft tissue in their left hand. To the Order, left signifies Satan. I believe they'll use the same technique the legend says they used in the Middle Ages to disperse the plague. Forty couriers of death, deployed to major cities around the world. The important question is how and where they'll bring the three components together."

"Boston or Sydney, I would think," Wethers answered immediately. "I suspect it will be in one of their facilities where they may have hidden passageways and escape tunnels."

"Good thought," Kurtzman spoke from the end of the table. "I agree. And if you were loosing a pandemic disease onto the world, would you select as its breakout point an isolated island continent where more than ninety percent of the land is sparsely populated?"

"Boston," everyone said together.

Kurtzman gave an approving nod to Price before addressing the rest of his cybernetics team by saying, "Your assignment is to search for all priests, monks or brothers who came into this country in the previous year. We have access to the billions of files Homeland Security uses in airports for biometric identification."

He shifted in his wheelchair to look directly at Tokaido. "Let's see if you can rewrite the FBI's comparison algorithms to search for marks on travelers' left hands instead of the characteristic facial points the recognition programs are currently set to analyze. It's going to be difficult because the source cameras are configured to record faces only."

Tokaido's frown indicated he thought his boss had just insulted him.

"How are you doing on Cafard, by the way?" Kurtzman asked.

The hacker's frown deepened, and he abruptly ceased bobbing his head in time to the rock music streaming from his MP3 player. It was the most subdued Bolan had ever seen the supertalented hacker, and he leaned forward in his chair to hear the reply.

"I need more time."

"To break French encryption?" Delahunt asked, her voice laced with a combination of concern and amazement. "You've gotten into Interpol records easily before."

"That's not it. There's a loose end," Tokaido said.

"Let me know if you want me to help," Delahunt replied.

Tokaido nodded, but Delahunt knew her cohort would exhaust himself by spending every waking moment in front of his keyboard. She made a mental note to mention to Kurtzman that if researching Cafard became a critical element in the case, they could not let pride get in the way of mission assurance.

As if he could read her thoughts, Brognola said, "I don't want a background check on Cafard to take precedence over anything else we're doing. As I said last week, I just don't like the guy. But the President told me to keep him informed.

"Striker's renovation project on one of their country's ancient abbeys hasn't been attributed to an American, so it probably never will. That's good, because I told you the President is concerned about our current relationship with France. I just wanted to know a little bit more about Cafard, that's all. I don't like reporting things that go on here to anyone outside. Needless to say, I'm not giving him a lot of detail."

"Could he be the leak?" Bolan asked.

Brognola narrowed his eyes and peered into the distance as if trying to remember exactly what he had told the man from Sentinelles. "I don't think so. He's a respected scientist within the French community. What would be his motivation to help launch a disease that could spread like wildfire throughout the entire world?" Brognola asked.

"Soon," Tokaido replied, "I'll tell you about him." But his brow was creased, and Bolan knew he wasn't telling the team the extent of the problems he was encountering.

"Before we break," Bolan said as his teammates began gathering their notes and preparing to leave, "I have a question, Hal."

The Stony Man team stopped what they were doing to pay attention. When Bolan took the time to question Brognola at one of their status meetings, it was never a trivial matter.

"Why, if we think Boston may be the site where the final weapon will be assembled," he asked, "don't we just storm the place with a combined force of Homeland Security, FBI and Boston police?"

"You're gonna love this," Brognola answered in a wry voice from the side of his mouth. "The land the Order of Raphael's facility is built on belongs to the French embassy. Even though the Order took out a one-hundred-year lease from the embassy when they moved there back in the sixties, everything within is protected by international laws dictating diplomatic immunity. Technically speaking, that building is on French soil. I posed the very same question to the President, but because it's France, he said we'd better make damn sure we have an ironclad case before we request his approval for a public action."

"So my probe the night before last—"

"Just a random burglar," Brognola interrupted before Bolan had a chance to finish his question. "Which, you may find interesting, was never reported to the police."

9

The brothers kissed each other on both cheeks as they always did upon meeting.

"Thank you for making time in your schedule to see me. I know as the day of prophecy draws near your presence is required elsewhere."

Abbot Gabriel gazed lovingly at his companion. "It is I who am grateful for your company," he said.

"How are you?"

The abbot shrugged, looking suddenly old and frail at the question. "Modern science works its wonders. And the Lord has shown us the way to use science against the Americans. The nation of sinners shall be brought low, and the Almighty shall smite our enemies."

"The soldier of the Beast has been unable to stop your project?"

"His warfare has seriously delayed us."

"He's on his way now to Australia."

Abbot Gabriel looked into the distance, his mouth drawn in a thin line. "The Lord has slowed His enemies to enable our success. The soldier of the Beast will arrive too late. I received word yesterday that MacPherson has finished his portion. The shipment will depart the continent despite the mighty forces the powers of evil summon."

"And you?"

"I'll travel to Boston as planned, where the power of the Lord's avenging angels will come together to smite the wicked. But the Almighty has seen fit to try my patience. We're approximately three weeks behind schedule. You must also adjust your calendar to reflect the actual release that will bring the whore of Babylon to her knees."

"I understand, Abbot Gabriel," he replied, showing respect by addressing the abbot by his new name. "I will not unveil the antidote until the proper time."

The abbot held his companion with his eyes for a few moments before saying, "You must adhere to the exact hour before bringing forth salvation to the world. One year, one month and one day from when the first of the Forty Martyrs are dispatched. The Lord has smiled on His faithful in France. From her hands mankind will be saved, restoring her to her former prestige. Blessed are those who are invited to the marriage supper of the Lamb."

Gabriel's companion swallowed hard, perhaps anticipating the abbot's reaction to the question he was about to pose. "But what if, dear Abbot, forgive me for asking, what if the plague leaps beyond North American boundaries? If it spreads to Europe or Asia, shall we stand idly by as it wipes out humanity? Or shall I provide the antidote sooner if the pandemic rages out of control?"

"Get thee behind me!" Gabriel replied angrily. "You and I are doing the work of God! Do you think any of what we have been through has been by chance? The attack with weapons and funding provided by the Americans? The exact timing of that attack?"

He reached forward to grab the other man by his arm for emphasis before continuing with the question. He asked in a slightly softer voice, "My needs that only you could satisfy? If the plague spreads out of control, it is God's will that it do so. You must mark your calendar to the exact hour in accordance with His word."

Gabriel's companion sighed and said in a heavy voice, "I will do your bidding." With a slight crack evident below the surface of his voice, he asked, "Shall I see you again?"

"Let us go in peace," was the abbot's answer as he made the sign of the cross in the space between them, and his visitor turned to depart. Tears filled the man's eyes with the knowledge that the next time they met face-to-face, it would be for eternity.

10

The very thought of a trip requiring twenty-four hours of flight time would make even the most seasoned traveler cringe. Throughout his career, Mack Bolan had flown thousands upon thousands of cumulative hours, and the ones he recalled disliking the most were not measured in terms of time or distance, but by the amount of incoming lead flying through the air in close proximity to his vital organs. Compared to a five-minute combat swoop into a hot zone while crouching in the open bay of a UH-1H Huey helicopter, a twenty-four-hour flight from New York to Sydney while occupying one of the fourteen first-class seats on a Boeing 747-400 operated by Qantas Airlines was a piece of cake.

Bolan knew as long as he kept himself hydrated by drinking a bottle of water every hour, and remembered to do isometric exercises and get in a few walks back and forth the entire length of the jumbo jet, the long flight time would not significantly degrade his performance.

On more than a dozen occasions, Bolan had jumped off a commercial airliner after completing an all-day flight and within hours found himself engaged in a raging firefight with no noticeable disintegration to his survival skills. But he was not anticipating serious efficiency problems reaching his hotel and picking up some hardware once his flight to Australia touched down at Sydney Airport.

Built on a strip of land jutting into Botany Bay, Australia's international airport was located approximately six miles south of the Central Business District, the main commerce area referred to as "The CBD" by city dwellers. It would take less than half an hour to get to the middle of the city from the airport. Bolan's appointment with LaFontaine wasn't until the next morning, which gave him a few hours of totally free time.

It was winter in the Southern Hemisphere, but it had been more than a century since snow had fallen onto Sydney streets. Situated on a coastal basin with the Pacific Ocean to its east and the Blue Mountains to its west, the city of four million people enjoyed the temperance of an oceanic climate. Winter temperatures averaged from a maximum of sixty-three degrees Fahrenheit to a minimum of forty-eight degrees.

As the plane made its final approach to the airport at Botany Bay, it flew directly over the famous Opera House situated on Sydney Harbour, and Bolan was impressed, as he always was whenever he flew to Australia, at how compact the capital city was. With a good portion of Sydney's available land already dedicated to parks and botanical gardens when the architects began rebuilding the business district following World War II, there wasn't much room for expansion. The result ended up being the Central Business District with skyscrapers erected more densely together than those on Manhattan.

Residential neighborhoods were literally blocks away, making Sydney one of those cities where its residents most often either walked or used efficient public transportation.

Both the Monorail and the tram ran on time and provided reliable service for use by workers, tourists and visitors to and from the inner-city suburbs neighboring the CBD.

Upon landing, Bolan grabbed his bag containing three changes of clothing from the overhead bin and hustled down the walkway toward customs. He was traveling light because he didn't plan on being in country for long.

Barbara Price had told him that the man who had checked out MacPherson's apartment, an intellectual operative named LaFontaine who was fluent in a number of languages, would be able to get him an interview with Richard Hannigan, a member of the normally reclusive JASON organization who had also been MacPherson's research deputy. Discussing the danger resulting from MacPherson's mouse pox work, and determining if Hannigan had been in touch with his colleague since his disappearance three or four weeks ago, was what Bolan considered his mission's objectives.

With a sixth sense honed on the unforgiving fields of combat, where an incorrect hunch most often led to death, the soldier believed that his enemy's forces were massing in the suburban Boston area. It was in the heavily populated cities of New England, he felt in his gut, not Sydney or Bayonne, that the decisive battle of this war would be fought.

As he expected to, Bolan breezed through customs. Barbara Price and Hal Brognola had set him up with an arms dealer named Albert Dunn who owned a furniture store specializing in American Shaker reproductions. Dunn's establishment was located in a suburb called Ultimo, which lay southwest of Sydney's CBD within walking distance from the hotel where Bolan was staying. As he left the airport, he decided he'd check into his hotel first, and immediately try to set up a meeting with Dunn. Once he was armed, he'd feel more comfortable walking through a foreign city. Then he'd call LaFontaine to set the appointment with JASON member Richard Hannigan.

THE WEATHER WAS SIMILAR to late autumn in Virginia, and dressed in black pants and the same dark blue windbreaker with its special panel tailored into the left shoulder section he had worn in Boston, Bolan decided to walk rather than use the Monorail or tram. Once he obtained his hardware, there was no question he would not be using public transportation for his return trip, despite the fact that museum station was conveniently located less than a block from his hotel room. In a post 9/11 world, the soldier sometimes would walk even considerable distances when he was packing serious heat rather than take the chance of being caught in a random checkpoint by local law-enforcement officials.

Walking west on Liverpool Street through the center of town, Bolan took in the sights and sounds of the multicultural city that drew visitors from all over the world. Australians as a people were fiercely independent, taking pride in a country that progressed from being one of the British Empire's most oppressed colonies to a nation that genuinely embraced diversity as a strength rather than a liability. As he made his way along the entire length of Liverpool Street, coming to a dead end at the Chinese Gardens adjacent to the Sydney Exhibition Centre, fellow pedestrians made eye contact, smiled and spoke to him with friendly greetings.

From the Chinese Gardens, it was a short walk to the western inner-city suburb named Ultimo, where Albert Dunn managed his furniture shop. On the outside, Dunn's establishment resembled its neighbors. Ultimo was apparently a section of town frequented by builders and professionals in the building or home renovation trades, as a plumbing supply store flanked Dunn's shop on one side, a high-tech appliance boutique on the other. Two doors down, an electronics store displaying a huge high-density plasma television screen had drawn a crowd of college-aged people who gestured and cheered loudly at the soccer match being pulled in via satellite dishes sprouting above the store's roof.

When he entered Dunn's store, Bolan's ears and nose were accosted with the smells and sounds associated with turning timber into fine furniture. The front section was a large open room with finished pieces such as bookcases, tables and chairs of various sizes and shapes, and occasional pieces ranging from end tables to sideboards. Although the furniture varied greatly both in size as well as the colors and textures of wood, every creation had remained true to the American Shaker dictate that function was plain, and plain was godly.

A salesman approached, eyeing him as if he knew before they spoke that Bolan was neither a local nor a potential customer.

"May I help you find something, sir?" he asked.

"I'm here for a meeting with Albert Dunn. Is he in right now?"

"Whom may I say is calling, please? Mr. Dunn usually does not help customers select pieces, you see. As owner, he has so many other responsibilities, he usually—"

Bolan interrupted the salesman in midsentence with a curt, "Tell him Matthew Cooper is here."

The salesman drew back as if he had never been interrupted before. With a look admonishing Bolan for a rudeness that in his world was simply intolerable, he turned abruptly on his heel and left to get his boss, exiting through a door at the rear of the showroom. Minutes later he reappeared with a man Bolan assumed to be Albert Dunn. The salesman pointed to his rude visitor and said a few words to the man with him before walking to the far side of the showroom where he could offer assistance to arriving customers who presumably would be better mannered.

Albert Dunn was a heavyset man who led with his stomach, at first glance appearing to be the type of man who never missed an opportunity to throw his weight into a barroom brawl. Thick curly black hair covered his head and the back of his neck to the frayed collar of his flannel shirt, and the forearms protruding from his rolled-up sleeves were muscular and well-toned. Despite the awkward amble Dunn's overextended belly caused as he approached, Bolan thought the man might display a surprising agility when engaged in a fight.

"Albert Dunn," he said, staring into Bolan's eyes with a confident intensity as they shook hands.

Returning his stare, Bolan replied, "Matt Cooper. I'm looking for a table made of yellow wood. Perhaps something the color of a canary?"

At the arranged mention of Barbara Price's code word, a flutter of recognition flashed behind Dunn's eyes.

"We have many types of wood," he replied, using the exact words Bolan was expecting, "in many colors and textures to meet every need."

"May I have a private showing?" Bolan asked.

"Indeed. Your timing is perfect, as I've recently restocked the inventory."

The agreed-upon code having been recited and answered

to the satisfaction of both parties, Dunn motioned with his head for Bolan to follow him through the door he had used to enter the showroom.

Dunn's furniture shop was laid out like a factory's assembly line. The workroom immediately behind the front showroom was filled with completed pieces being finished and buffed to final perfection before making their way to the sales area on the other side of the wall. Three men were applying stains and varnishes to assembled pieces, while a fourth was using an electric buffer to polish the top of a table on which the varnish had dried and hardened.

Bolan and Dunn walked quickly through the finishing area into an assembly room that stank of glue and turpentine before progressing to the back end of the building where table saws buzzed and sawdust filled the air as raw wood underwent the first step in the transformation from timber to fine furniture.

Dunn's office was at the very back of the store, a windowless square that appeared to have been added to the interior space as an afterthought. Dunn locked the door behind them, then pushed his desk a few feet from where it occupied a good portion of the tiny room crowded with file cabinets and straight-backed chairs. He kicked away a cheap imitation Persian rug, exposing a trapdoor. Grunting loudly as he bent, Dunn grabbed the door's handle and pulled the door open. Steep wooden stairs led almost straight down to the basement.

Dunn went first, reaching for a light switch when he was shoulder deep into the cellar. Bolan followed him into a cool concrete room lined with bookcases displaying the same style and quality he had seen in the showroom at the front of the store. Every shelf was occupied with weapons of a variety Bolan had rarely seen from a private dealer.

In the harsh bare-bulb glare of the basement lighting, Dunn turned and asked, "What are we looking for t'day, mate?"

"Desert Eagle and a Beretta 93-R," Bolan replied.

Dunn shook his head in a short quick denial. "Don't have either. Let's see what we can do."

He took a few steps, reached above his head to a shelf and brought down a blue velvet lined tray on which a Pardini MP semiautomatic pistol lay like a rare gem a jeweler might display to his very finest customers. In the center of the room, with barely enough space to walk between it and the shelves, was a simple occasional table, its surface waist-high to Bolan. Dunn placed the tray on the table and glanced at his customer, eyebrows raised expectantly.

"Too small," Bolan said, referring to the weapon's .32-caliber rounds. "I need at least 9 mm."

"Okay," Dunn said, replacing the tray. "Then I won't even show you the Walthers or Benellis."

He moved toward the shelves on the opposite wall of the tiny cellar, with Bolan following. When they were a few steps away, a weapon caught Bolan's eye. A pair of Spectre submachine guns sat on display. The Italian wonder gun, less than fourteen inches long with its stock folded, was capable of feeding 9 mm slugs from a specially designed 50-round box magazine at 850 rpm.

"This is more like it," Bolan said, taking one of the weapons off the shelf.

Dunn smiled appreciatively, the way a wine steward might at a diner's unexpected selection of the precisely correct vintage.

"Indeed. I have standard and hollowpoint ammo. Already stacked in the 50-round magazines. All you want."

"I'll take them both," Bolan answered, "with five mags for each. Hollowpoint."

He placed the two submachine guns on the table while Dunn reached to the back of a shelf and retrieved ten box magazines, hefting them onto the table next to the guns.

"Will you be needing a backup piece? Here, let me show you something similar to the Desert Eagle you requested."

The arms dealer reached to another shelf and brought down a Heckler & Koch Mk.23 pistol with a shoulder holster on which four leather loops were stitched to hold extra 12-round magazines.

"If you like this, I have ACP plus P," he said, referring to the enhanced ammunition the Mk.23 had been designed to accommodate. The .45-caliber ACP+P cartridges were full-metal-jacketed 185-grain truncated cone slugs, which, due to the ammo's higher pressure and muzzle velocity, enabled greater accuracy than what was normally achievable with standard .45 rounds.

"Yeah," Bolan said. "I've used these before. Ten clips? One hundred twenty of the ACP plus P?"

"Done. Commo?"

"Wait, before we leave the HK. Do you have a silencer?"

"Thread or bayonet?"

Because he believed that gases—and thus sound—had more of a chance escaping from a bayonet push-and-twist mount than a threaded sound suppressor, he preferred to use the latter, and told Dunn so.

"Got it. Commo?" he repeated.

Bolan didn't know enough about LaFontaine to know his preference, so he replied, "Earpiece with jaw mike. Closed frequency."

"Okay. Night-vision goggles?"

"Two pair. XR-5s?"

"Nothing but the best," Dunn said with a grin.

No mention was made of payment. Dunn grabbed a large canvas duffel bag from a pile of four or five similar ones stacked in the corner, tossed it onto the table and was loading Bolan's hardware into it when the Executioner asked, "Do you have plastique?"

Dunn stopped what he was doing in order to turn to face his customer. "I do indeed," he replied, a smile touching the corners of his mouth. "C-4."

"What kind of fuses?"

"Individual or group?"

"Group," Bolan replied immediately, indicating he had already formulated a plan involving the simultaneous detonation of multiple chunks of C-4 plastic explosive.

"Number two blasting cap with microchip fuse. RF detonator, no delay, low end freq."

"Yeah. Two bricks?" Bolan asked, referring to the way the gray compound, was packaged in sticks roughly the same size and shape as butter.

Dunn walked to a filing cabinet in one corner, opened the bottom drawer, and took out a combat knife similar to the Fairbairn-Sykes model Bolan often carried on missions. After reaching behind the cabinet, the arms dealer came back holding the combat knife in one hand and a solid gray pipe about six feet long and as thick as Bolan's thumb in the other. He placed the tube on the table, and beginning at one end, moved the knife slowly up the length.

"Say when," he said to Bolan as if he was a waiter grinding pepper corns from a crank mill onto a tossed green salad instead of an international weapons dealer slicing off a length of high-explosive plastique capable of blowing a building clean off its foundation.

"There," Bolan told him. "Four like that."

Dunn sliced the knife through the explosive, then used the first length as a template for three additional pieces. He placed the remaining length on end back behind the file cabinet. Next he returned the knife to the bottom drawer and withdrew a plastic bag containing four blasting caps and a small detonator resembling a USB flash drive.

"Trigger the detonator here," he said, touching a tiny lever next to the hot button that, once slid through a channel running the entire length of the unit about the size of an automobile's alarm remote, would activate a specific transmission frequency matching the one programmed into the blasting caps' microchips. "It needs downward pressure to slide."

Bolan nodded. He had used similar devices with safety precautions built into the detonator's design to prevent the blasting caps from accidentally exploding while they were still in their plastic bags.

Dunn finished loading Bolan's hardware into the duffel bag, led him back up the steep stairs into the business office, and showed him out the furniture shop's back door to a narrow alley littered with cigarette butts and crushed paper cups leading onto Mary Ann Street.

"My best to your contact," he said as he shook hands with Bolan. "Always a pleasure doing business with her, it is."

Bolan hefted the duffel bag over his right shoulder and stepped into the cool afternoon air for the forty-five-minute jaunt back to his hotel. Once there, he would make contact with LaFontaine for the morning's meeting.

11

Bolan and LaFontaine were sitting on a wrought-iron bench situated a few yards off one of the numerous pedestrian paths running through the eastern edge of Sydney's Royal Botanic Gardens. Bolan had picked that specific location because it was more forested than the park's western edge, which bordered the Central Business District. They were almost directly across the gardens from Australia's Conservatorium of Music. Because it was mid-morning on a workday, there was no one else in the immediate area.

From his spot, Bolan could see through the trees and across a portion of Farm Cove, the wide U-shaped inlet with a walking path immediately adjacent to the water. The trail stretched all the way from Mrs. Macquaries Chair to the Man O' War stairs leading directly to the Sydney Opera House. Except for the final few yards, where the trail ended on the grounds of the famous multipeaked performance center, the walkway hugged the entire shoreline of Farm Cove without once straying more than a few steps from the surf. Pedestrians using the path were treated throughout the entire distance to spectacular views of the Opera House and Sydney Harbour, resulting in the smooth flat walkway being crowded year-round with tourists enjoying the sights against a sparkling backdrop of the CBD's modern skyscrapers.

A morning breeze, cool and salty, was gusting inland off the water, ruffling Bolan's thick black hair. Concealed under his dark blue windbreaker, in a brown leather holster strapped to his left shoulder, he carried the Mk.23 automatic assault pistol he had picked up the day before from Dunn. A 12-round magazine was locked and loaded into its ammo port. The pistol's sound suppressor, which effectively doubled the length of the weapon, was attached to the barrel's end. When Bolan leaned forward, he could feel the end of the suppressor rubbing uncomfortably against his rib cage, but the feel of a handgun, while not as reassuring as the comfort provided by either his Beretta 93-R or Desert Eagle, was nonetheless an improvement over being unarmed.

"Are they sure it's MacPherson?" Bolan asked in response to the information LaFontaine had just given him.

"Absolutely," the field agent answered without looking his way. "Bastards shot him in the back of the head. I hope someone that smart never saw it coming. One of the world's top scientists. Funny they would leave the body where it was sure to be found, don't you think?" He sighed heavily and added, "What a freakin' shame."

LaFontaine was in his midthirties, with a reputation for being an intellectual in the office, and somewhat reckless in the field.

"You've set up the meeting with Richard Hannigan?" Bolan asked.

"Yeah," LaFontaine replied. "We're picking him up at noon. We'll bring him over to our place."

"I want to talk to him alone," Bolan said.

"I know," LaFontaine answered. "I'll drop him off."

The field operatives working throughout the world for the Sensitive Operations Group were not official members of any government sanctioned organization such as the FBI or CIA, but in the years immediately following the 9/11 attacks, the entire intelligence community had cooperated to establish a loose coalition that often shared resources and facilities without poking their noses into each other's business. The place LaFontaine referred to was actually a CIA safehouse on Ormond Street in the southeast inner-city suburb of Paddington.

"What about tonight?" LaFontaine asked. "This was supposed to be a search and rescue, wasn't it? Too late for that now."

"I say we go in anyway," Bolan replied in a firm voice. "I have plastique and two Spectre subguns. We'll take down the entire organization."

LaFontaine uttered a short nervous laugh and said, "Count me in on that one. The Italian zappers? Yeah. How much ammo do you have?"

"Five boxes each."

A strange smile was spreading across LaFontaine's face as he looked at dozens of small craft tacking westerly courses on the water, their crisp white sails standing out in sharp contrast against the turquoise Pacific Ocean. When he looked back at Bolan, his eyes were gleaming as if lit from behind by a raging fire.

"Do we want tracers?" he asked in an excited way that made Bolan remember what people had told him about La-Fontaine being a bit wild when the lead started flying. "Just think of it," he continued. "Dead of night, pitch black, every fourth or fifth round is a tracer. Set up converging fire and right from the get-go, we'll scare the freakin' bejesus out of 'em!"

Bolan had used tracers often enough throughout his career to understand the psychological impact the red laser-crisp lines had on the enemy. Zipping through the black night air as if their source was an alien weapon, tracers transformed nighttime firefights into a surrealistic nightmare.

When the enemy was caught in converging fire with tracer-laced rounds incoming from weapons shattering the still of night with eardrum throbbing full-auto chatter, the terror was horrific. Bolan understood that and nodded in agreement. "How far outside the city is their place?" he asked.

LaFontaine thought for a long moment while he stroked the side of his face the way a man did when deciding if he needed a shave. "It's not the outback, but they're way the hell off the beaten path. Heading toward Berowra, it'll take us—" he paused and screwed up one side of his face "—about an hour and a half, maybe two hours to get there. No one will hear us out there, that's for sure."

"They may know I'm coming," Bolan said.

"Have any of the members seen your face?"

"None that lived, but when I—"

Bolan stopped in midsentence, his hand slipping into the front of his windbreaker.

LaFontaine followed his gaze, his own hand mimicking Bolan's movement as the agent found the handle of his SIG-Sauer P-229 semiautomatic pistol.

Because their bench was off the walking path a few yards into the woods, Bolan and LaFontaine had not yet been spotted by the three men who were treading softly through the trees approximately one hundred yards away. It was obvious they were searching for someone. Were it not for the deep maroon port-wine stain covering half the face of the lead man, Bolan may not have noticed them until they had drawn much closer.

An image flashed through his mind of Dr. Zagorski's rescue from the lab at the abbey in Bayonne. After taking the unconscious guard's FHN P-90 submachine gun, they had shoved him up against the wall where he'd be out of their line of fire. Amazingly, he had survived not only the hail of bullets that peppered the laboratory for minutes without pause, he had also lived through the hurricane explosion of glass that had to have sent shards into every inch of that room when Bolan's concussion grenade detonated.

"He doesn't have to die," Zagorski had said, and Bolan had agreed. At the time, it was the right decision. The unconscious guard had posed no threat to the Executioner's mission accomplishment.

"Those three?" LaFontaine asked without moving an inch.

They both understood that sudden motion would draw the eyes of the enemy directly to their position.

"Yeah. They'll probably have FN Five-seveNs."

"I don't wear Kevlar anyway," LaFontaine answered, sliding in ultra slow motion off the bench to the ground. "Your piece silenced?"

"Yeah," Bolan replied.

Bolan followed the field agent's example, joining him on the lush grass carpet running through the entire gardens, lightly blanketed in this heavily treed section with a thin layer of fragrant pine needles. From there, they low-crawled into the cover of the dense spruce woods behind the walking path. Once they were out of sight, each man rose to a crouch before setting a course to intersect the trio. Every now and then they took a moment to sneak to the edge of their cover in order to check their enemies' position.

"Let's try to take them alive," Bolan said as they jogged through the deserted woods.

"We'll see."

It was a reply the Executioner interpreted as meaning head shots from round one.

"We need their intel. Let's try to take them alive," he repeated firmly.

"You're right," LaFontaine answered after a brief hesitation. "We'll take at least one alive."

As they moved south through the gardens, with Woolloomooloo Bay on their left, the woods became more dense. Bolan was grateful the forest was predominately spruce and cedar. Although the weather was not severe, the indigenous trees experienced a biological cycle of growth and defoliation similar to those in Virginia. Had the park been populated with maples, oaks, and elm, Bolan knew that he and his partner would be scrambling for concealment behind naked branches like the ones found in December on trees in Vermont when a hunter can see for a mile through the woods.

The forest reached its thickest point just north of the Cahill Expressway, which marked the dividing line between the Royal Botanic Gardens and the Domain, an equally impressive expanse of well-tended parkland in front of Australia's Parliament House and State Library. Before Bolan and LaFontaine got that far, the trio they were stalking changed their bearing to take them into the woods.

"Ambush!" Bolan said, slipping off to the right to a po-

sition behind a clump of cedars while LaFontaine hustled
to move to a spot fifty yards distant.

"Let them get past us," LaFontaine whispered over his
shoulder as if his companion would not realize the implica-
tion of a kill zone defined by direct cross fire.

While he waited in the peaceful solitude of the cedar
grove, Bolan pondered how the Order could have known he
was meeting with LaFontaine. Barbara Price had told him
that the ancient legend said God sent visions to the Order's
abbot during crucial times. Over the years he had seen a lot
of strange things in a lot of strange places, but Bolan didn't
believe for one second that the abbot at the Order of Raphael
was getting his intel from the man upstairs. It was much
more likely that one of Brognola's contact organizations
had been infiltrated. Bolan fully intended to root out and kill
the traitor responsible for placing him at risk. Before he
considered this case closed, he would permanently plug the
leak.

The three Order members were attempting to be quiet,
but it was obvious that none of the men had been trained to
be combat soldiers, and stealth was not one of their natural
strong points. From behind the cedar grove, Bolan peered
through the branches and patiently watched them approach.

They had drawn their weapons upon entering the deserted woods, knowing they were beyond the sight of the
few tourists who happened to be in various sections of the
park away from the ocean where almost all the visitors at
this time of year were drawn.

Bolan let them pass his spot, waiting until they were approximately ten yards distant before taking a few steps forward and shouting in a hard voice that left no room for
negotiation, "Drop the guns. Get your hands up now!"

All three spun in his direction, and with the instincts of a battle-tested veteran, Bolan launched himself into a dive that propelled him back behind the cover of the cedars. A flurry of 5.7 mm rounds snapped through the air where he had been an instant earlier as he landed hard.

He rolled as soon as he landed and triggered his Mk.23 in response. As they exited the business end of the pistol's sound suppressor, the enhanced bullets made a coughing sound very similar to that of the 9 mm rounds from his silenced Beretta. His first shot hit the gunman on the far right in his upper thigh, and the man dropped his pistol as he fell to the ground, screaming in pain. Twisting in agony while he clutched his leg with both hands as if attempting to stem the tide of gushing blood that soaked his pants, he turned a smooth clean face toward Bolan. The young man's eyes rolled upward, his eyelids fluttered and he lapsed into unconsciousness.

The other two scrambled away, frantically diving for cover. The one with the port-wine stain across half his face found refuge behind a pile of rocks, the other hid on the far side of a clump of tress similar to the cedars shielding Bolan.

The guard from Bayonne raised his head to get a view above the rocks, his eyes darting back and forth in search of Bolan.

Off to his left, Bolan heard the muffled retort of LaFontaine's SIG-Sauer coughing twice, and the portion of the gunman's head exposed above the pile of rocks exploded in a crimson cloud of bone chips and gore. As if the rest of his body was attempting to remain with the top of his skull, the corpse flew three feet to the rear of the rock pile, where it lay absolutely still but for the quick pulses of blood from a gaping hole above his eyebrows.

The other gunman, realizing he was facing two superior foes, ill-advisedly chose to fight his way to better cover, perhaps hoping that a more advantageous position would afford him the opportunity to escape. He jumped from behind the cover of the trees, the FN Five-seveN pistol blazing in his right hand. Bolan was a millisecond away from placing a .45-caliber round into the shoulder of his firing arm when LaFontaine's SIG-Sauer spit a 9-mm message of death.

The man jerked upright for a second and appeared as if he was about to speak, but any sound that may have been forthcoming was instantly drowned by the geyser of blood that rushed in a torrent through his nose and mouth from a severed carotid artery. His forward momentum carried him a few steps closer to his wounded companion before he collapsed in a heap onto the ground.

Bolan shoved his Mk.23 into his shoulder holster and sprinted forward to the man holding his thigh, quickly patting him down for additional weapons. When he was sure his unconscious victim was clean, he tore open the leg of the man's pants where the bullet had entered. Using his teeth, he ripped free a long strip of cloth, grabbed a short stick about twice the thickness of his thumb and quickly fashioned a field tourniquet.

LaFontaine was a few steps behind, talking a mile a minute into his cell phone while sucking in quick, raspy gulps of air. The glassy sheen of his eyes and the flush of blood coloring his cheeks a bright pink as he ran forward to join Bolan told the combat veteran that the agent was pumped on adrenaline.

As he closed the cell phone and casually slipped it into his pocket, he looked over at Bolan. "What?" he asked.

"I said alive!" Bolan shouted.

"We said one."

There was an awkward silence between them as Bolan drilled the field agent with his eyes while LaFontaine's hurried breathing returned to normal.

"Okay," he said with a downcast look. "My bad." He remained silent for a long moment before saying, "You'd better get out of here in case the local police arrive before our people do. We have a relationship with them, but I think it's best if you're not here."

Bolan stood and said, "I don't want anyone touching this guy until I get there, understand?"

LaFontaine nodded. "Okay."

The wounded man began moaning softly as Bolan continued talking.

"No advance questions, no pain, get him medical treatment and make him as comfortable as possible. No drugs."

"I said okay."

Bolan took a few steps before turning back and repeating, "No pain, no drugs."

"I heard you," LaFontaine answered. "I'm not freakin' deaf!"

12

The CIA safehouse in the southeast inner-city suburb of Paddington looked like every other house Bolan passed as he made his way through the well-maintained neighborhood. The three-story residence, designed to resemble a classic country farmhouse, was in keeping with the architecture of the bordering properties, with weathered cedar shakes on the exterior capped by a Federalist roof constructed of hammered tin.

Features not evident from the outside included a double brick wall, eight inches thick, fabricated between the exterior siding and interior plaster; a communications antenna concealed in the attic that maintained constant contact with satellites in geocentric orbit; a bank of high-frequency noise generators that enveloped the house in an electronic umbrella preventing outsiders from eavesdropping on anything occurring within, and steel plates one-inch thick mounted on slides inside the walls above the windows and doors, ready to descend into place at a moment's notice if conditions suddenly arose requiring the house to be transformed into a fortress.

Across the street from the safehouse, a woman wearing a straw hat with a brim broad enough to shade her entire face was tending a bed of perennial flowers, trimming dead sprigs to ready the plants for the upcoming spring season. Although she was very discreet, the instincts that had kept Bolan alive warned him that the neighbor was not what she appeared to be. As he approached the safehouse, he surveyed her with his peripheral vision, never looking directly her way, but noticing that her movements were not as efficient as a true gardener's might be. She lingered a bit long over the ends of the plants before pruning them back, taking the time to study and cut them to precisely the correct length.

Bolan had seen horticulturists perform the same task with a zeal bordering on mayhem, and knew the correct process was to simply wade into the growth and hack it back in a manner often appearing to a nongardener to be haphazard. The woman across the street was employing too neat and exact a technique. Bolan also noted that the straw tote bag sitting on the ground within easy reach was of a size more suited to hold a handgun than gardening clippers and shears. As he reached his destination, he was reminded of the field hands at Stony Man Farm whose coveralls concealed automatic pistols they carried while tending the fields surrounding the Farm's main buildings. With the woman being out in the open directly across the street from the safehouse, he was sure those within knew who she was.

Bolan strolled casually up the multicolored flagstone walk bisecting a neatly trimmed front lawn that set the safehouse back fifty feet from the sidewalk. At the end of the walkway, he took the six steps leading to a wraparound porch two at a time. The porch floorboards were stained a light color to enhance the pattern of the yellow wood's grain, and the ceiling was painted a robin's-egg blue, creating a soft ambiance. Half a dozen wicker chairs and love seats held thick cushions and pillows made of brightly colored fabric printed in a large flowery pattern. The informal arrangement of the chairs positioned with matching wicker tables created the impression that in good weather, the porch was probably a place where the home owners often entertained or ate their meals.

There was a doorbell next to the front door, and Bolan pressed it with his index finger, aware that as he did so, his fingerprint was being transmitted to a bank of computers operating in the basement's temperature and humidity controlled environment. He'd make sure that Aaron Kurtzman hacked into the database and deleted it.

A voice sounding from a tiny speaker mounted into the porch's bead board ceiling directed him to place his entire hand on one of the front door panels. Bolan did so, and within seconds the door swung open on silent hinges to reveal a man dressed in khaki pants and a red-and-white-checkered flannel shirt.

"Good afternoon, Mr. Cooper," he said, extending his hand. As they shook hands, the man said, "Welcome. I'm Drew Thompson, the house manager. Please come inside."

Thompson was trim and muscular, with short hair and a thin blond mustache. His manner was congenial and confident, conveying the impression that he was in complete control of the house. The job of a CIA house manager was to eliminate the nuisances of mundane matters field operatives faced while accomplishing their missions. Thompson's specific service was to provide a reliable safe location for agents in Sydney to conduct business without having to think about anything other than those items pertinent to their objectives. Bolan immediately liked him, sensing after less than a minute that Thompson was a professional who performed his job to perfection.

As he stepped across the threshold, the door closed behind him, automatically locking with a slight sound of tumblers and dead bolts sliding into place. The foyer gave no indication of being anything other than a normal residence. To Bolan's left, there was a dining room with a glass chandelier suspended above a round table large enough for a family of six, and through the distant doorway, he could see a kitchen.

As if he could read Bolan's thoughts, Thompson said, "We have interrogation rooms up on second deck, and rooms outfitted to provide medical support on third. You currently have clients on both decks."

He paused for a second as if awaiting a confirming response or perhaps a question from Bolan. Upon receiving neither, he continued. "The man with the thigh wound is resting comfortably. He received medical treatment, with no drugs other than a painkiller being administered, and asked for a Bible, which I provided to him. He is secure, with no means available to commit suicide.

"Dr. Hannigan is awaiting you in one of our soundproof interrogation rooms. I must say he was a bit miffed at being brought here blindfolded, although Mr. LaFontaine assures me he knew in advance of the precautions we intended. With whom would you like to speak first?"

"Hannigan," Bolan said.

"Do you want your conversation recorded?"

"No. I'd like to have it sent real time to my contact in the States. I'll provide the security protocol."

"Right. We will encrypt and transmit it real time."

"Please do that for both my clients," Bolan said.

"Very well, sir. There's coffee, juice and water in the interrogation room, and notepads for your use. Let me know if there's anything else you need. This way please."

He led Bolan up a flight of stairs to a long hallway. Closed doors lined both sides of a center corridor, six rooms on each side.

"There's an intercom on the wall next to the door," Thompson said as he reached for one of the doorknobs. "When you're finished, please inform us by using the intercom. The door will be locked for entry, but you may exit at any time. I ask that you not do so without first letting me know."

He pulled the door open, and Bolan entered for his meeting with Richard Hannigan.

The virologist had brought a stack of trade journals with him, and was engrossed in reading an article when Bolan entered. The windowless room was furnished sparsely, and Bolan realized the window treatments seen from the street were nothing but facades. Against one wall, a sideboard was laden with the beverages Thompson had mentioned. Hannigan sat in one of four straight-back wooden chairs around a table in the center of the room, two eight-by-ten pads of yellow paper next to his journals. A cup of coffee set on a matching china saucer was a few inches to the left of the journals, a thin tendril of steam rising from the liquid's surface.

Hannigan appeared to be in his fifties or sixties, dressed in a forest green cardigan sweater over a plain white shirt buttoned all the way to his neck. He sported a full beard and wore half-moon reading glasses with silver frames, giving him the undeniable look of an academic. He glanced up, closed the journal and stood.

"Hello, I'm Matt Cooper," Bolan said as he advanced to the table. "Thank you for agreeing to see me. I apologize for the inconvenience our security may have caused, but we're dealing with a terrorist organization that murdered your friend and colleague."

"Then it's true?" Hannigan asked in a thin voice at least one octave above what Bolan was expecting. "What they told me when I got here? Terrance MacPherson is dead?"

"I believe so," Bolan replied.

Hannigan sighed heavily and sat down. Bolan pulled one of the wooden chairs away from the table and joined him.

"It could have been either of us," Hannigan said in a trembling voice. "Terrance and I lived in constant fear for our lives once our research was published. What began as such a promising project, to rid the continent of the recurring plague of mice, and then move on to mitigate the losses caused by the rabbits and rats, how could it have gone so wrong? How could it have…" His voice tapered off into silence.

He picked up the cup of coffee with a hand that displayed a slight tremor, blew softly on the surface and took a tiny sip.

"When was the last time you spoke to MacPherson?" Bolan asked.

The virologist put the cup down and stared at Bolan with clear blue eyes so pale they were almost colorless. "Oh, every day," he said as if surprised that Bolan didn't know the answer already. "Until a few days ago, and then I suspected the worst. He tried to delay his part of the project, but they tortured him. He was ashamed to be giving in to their demands, but Terrance was not good at handling pain."

Bolan leaned forward in his chair. "You talked with him while he was being held captive?" he asked incredulously.

Hannigan shook his head quickly. "Not exactly talked. As I said, we feared for our safety, but since there was no specific threat, it was nothing the police could help with. We often discussed this exact scenario! What would we do if we were taken captive by a terrorist group? So we worked out a code of sorts. A way of communicating."

Bolan leaned back, his mind filling with questions as Hannigan continued.

"It was one-way communication. Terrance could send me a message, but I could not reach him. To do our work, you see, we need access to computers and databases containing specific research. Results are published in journals such as these—" he motioned with a wave of his hand to the journals on the table before them "—and both Terrance and I hold editing authority for certain publications. Terrance's captors allowed him to retrieve required research, but his computer was not enabled to send."

He paused and took another sip of coffee while raising an eyebrow as if to ask if Bolan was following him thus far.

"Okay, he could download articles from journals, but he couldn't send anything out. I understand that, but how—"

Hannigan stopped the question by pressing the palm of his hand in the air between them.

"He could download articles, or portions of articles I was editing prior to publication," Hannigan said. "Because I held editing authority, I could see what people were downloading from the editing database. Similar to the way you can track changes in a word processing document. Terrance downloaded individual words from my articles that when strung together, created a message."

"Why didn't you go straight to the authorities?" Bolan asked.

When Hannigan answered, his eyes held a mixture of pain and guilt. "Because I feared for my friend's life, and neither of us believed they would actually kill him once he gave them what they wanted. They were not technologically savvy, and we thought we could defeat them by capitalizing on that weakness."

He paused for a second, during which the thought passed through Bolan's mind that there was a better, more permanent way to defeat the Order of Raphael.

Hannigan took a deep breath and continued almost as an afterthought, "And Terrance thought he might discover where they were keeping the antidote. I thought if I went to the police, they would kill him outright, and all would be lost."

"There's an antidote?" Bolan asked, resisting the urge to jump from his chair and shake the scientist.

"Oh, yes. Terrance's portion was designed to be the place where the antidote would attack the virus. The cure was developed in advance. They gave him exact parameters so that he would build his portion to be vulnerable to the antidote."

Bolan's mind was reeling with the information he was glad was being transmitted real time to Barbara Price.

"Where do you think the antidote is being stored?"

Hannigan shook his head slowly, frowning. "He didn't know. Bermuda perhaps."

"Bermuda? Why Bermuda?"

"That's where Terrance thought his portion was being flown. The target, you see, is the United States. Terrance believed the antidote was to keep it from spreading elsewhere."

"And how bad will it be?" Bolan asked, bracing himself for the reply.

Hannigan swallowed hard, ran a suddenly dry tongue over his lips and replied, "Statistically you could expect eighty percent of the population to contract the virus, which will be attached to a variant of the common cold. Greater than ninety percent will die within a week."

13

"I've got it, Striker."

Barbara Price's very first sentence upon answering his call told him she had been listening to his interview with Dr. Hannigan.

Bolan was sitting alone in one of Thompson's other interrogation rooms down the hall from where he had talked minutes earlier with Hannigan, conversing over an encrypted secure line. Half a world away, Price was in the climate-controlled Computer Room at Stony Man Farm, working with Aaron Kurtzman and his team.

The four computer geniuses were sitting at their workstations. As they wrote programs and crunched numbers, the large flat-screen monitor above each station reflected the work in row after row of data the cyberteam could read as easily as if it were prose. Their fingers flying at blurring speed over the keyboards, they created, tweaked and revised programs that were sifting through billions of pieces of information in the search for forty specific travelers from Europe.

Being unsure of both the departure and destination airports, the time frame of the flights, and the passengers' transportation arrangements following touch down, what they presumed was unfortunately much more than what they knew. As one program after another failed to down-select to a unique data set identifying a specific individual, Kurtzman and his team wrote new programs on the fly.

"Can we track the ships leaving Bermuda for Boston?" Bolan asked.

"Yes. Carmen and Akira both have background programs running now to find all flights originating from Sydney arriving in Bermuda for the past two weeks. From what Hannigan said, we know MacPherson was alive ten days ago. That will give us a more specific time window, although even with that, the task is daunting.

"From that first data set we'll focus in on ships coming to Boston. The assumption we're making is that the Order is bringing MacPherson's portion in by sea. They must have realized our docks are a lot less secure than our airports. Trying to smuggle even a portion of a bioweapon through airport customs is risky business. That's the only scenario that makes sense. It would take too long to come all the way by boat, but Bermuda is only a day's cruise from Boston."

"Boston, remember, is also only an assumption," Bolan said.

"This is a bad one," Price replied with an element of stress that came through the phone.

There was a sharp click on the line, and Hal Brognola asked, "When are you coming back, Striker?"

Bolan realized Price had to have conferenced in the man from the Justice Department as soon as she saw his call coming in from Australia.

"Tomorrow. With the statistical projections from Hannigan, can you convince the President to approve action on the Order's facility in Boston? I say we go in with or without his approval."

The hesitation an instant before Brognola answered his question set off an alarm in Bolan's mind.

"Too late, Striker. Homeland Security and the FBI, along with Boston police, hit the Order's site early this morning as soon as we learned that MacPherson's body had been found. Killing him was a loud and clear signal that his portion was done, and that scared the President into action. The place on Park Drive was empty."

Bolan could hear his heart thumping in his ears as he processed the implications of what Brognola was saying.

"What about Bayonne?"

The sound of Brognola exhaling heavily signaled the answer to the question. "The President shared everything we have, and Interpol raided L'Abbaye de Raphael less than an hour ago. Same as Boston. The monastery was deserted.

"Getting approval from the Australian government is taking longer than we expected, and we don't have enough people there to go in by ourselves in case it's still occupied and heavily defended. But I suspect that site, too, will be clean."

"LaFontaine and I are taking it as soon as it gets dark. They're still there. I have a prisoner," Bolan said.

"From the Order of Raphael?" Brognola asked.

Bolan related the episode in the Royal Botanic Gardens, ending his tale by presenting the theory that because MacPherson had only recently finished his assigned tasks, and because Australia was so far away, it was probably going to take the Order longer to break camp at their Sydney location.

"We'll have a team of specialists standing by to go into that lab as soon as you and LaFontaine clear whatever resistance is there," Brognola said.

"We know there were at least three of them out there this

morning," Bolan answered. "As soon as we finish here, I'm going up to question my prisoner."

"Pull all stops," Price said.

Her direction, with Brognola's tacit approval, conveyed to Bolan the degree of failure their cybernetics team at Stony Man Farm was experiencing.

"Does Thompson have access to a chemist?" Bolan asked, using CIA jargon for a doctor skilled at administering truth serum.

"No. Phil Lacey is our contact down there. Fortunately for us he's less than half an hour from your location. I'll get in touch with him. Patch me in real time again," Price said.

"Already done."

"Once we're on, I'll conference you in on your cell. I want two way talk on this one."

A FEW MINUTES BEFORE Dr. Phil Lacey arrived with a supply of truth serum, Bolan entered the room on the third floor of Thompson's safehouse where his prisoner lay with his ankles chained in padded cuffs to the foot of the bed.

"My name is Matt," Bolan said, "and I want you to know we will not hurt you."

The man was young, perhaps in his early to midtwenties, at an age when dying for a cause sometimes seemed to be noble. He closed the Bible he was reading, placed it on the nightstand next to the bed and eyed Bolan suspiciously.

Bolan's cell phone vibrated, and he flipped it open, turned on the internal speaker, and placed it on a straight-backed wooden chair next to the bed where it would be out of his prisoner's reach. An errant thought flashed through Bolan's mind that the chair was the same type he had seen in Dunn's furniture shop.

"Will you tell me your name?" Bolan asked.

The man thought for a moment before replying, "I am Brother Thomas, a member of the Order of Raphael. I am a man of God."

"A man of God who arms himself with an automatic pistol and comes with two others to commit murder? Somewhere in that book you were just reading there's a command that thou shalt not kill. Your Order is a misguided cult that's planning to commit murder on an unimaginable scale," Bolan said.

"No. Abbot Gabriel receives visions from God. He warned the Brothers in Boston when he saw you in a vision. He told us you were coming to Sydney. The time of the Revelation is at hand. Our calling is to do the work of the Almighty. I see through your guile. You are a soldier of the Beast, and you will be brought low by the power of the Lord."

There was a quick knock on the door, and a man carrying a black leather medical bag entered. Brother Thomas swallowed hard, and his eyes grew as large as saucers.

Bolan said, "I told you we will not hurt you. That's the truth. But this man is going to drug you in an attempt to save millions of lives. If your faith is strong enough, I guess you won't tell us what we want to know. Either way you won't remember this conversation or anything else from the previous three or four hours. Tomorrow you'll be turned over to the authorities and charged with involvement in a number of capital crimes."

"The Lord is my shepherd. I shall not want."

"You can make this easy or hard on yourself," Bolan said evenly. "If you struggle, I'll have someone come in and hold you down. How powerful is your faith, Brother Thomas?"

Bolan's words produced the desired effect. Thomas looked him unflinchingly in the eyes, and replied, "God Almighty will seal my mouth as He sealed the mouths of the lions in Daniel's den. Blessed are the dead who die in the name of the Lord."

With a nod to Phil Lacey, Bolan said, "You're not going to die."

Lacey opened his bag and produced a cup, two glass vials with screw-on caps and a cotton swab. After pulling on a pair of latex gloves, he opened one of the vials, drenched the cotton swab and wiped it against Thomas's forehead.

"This is just to cool you down a little," he said reassuredly. He stepped away, opened the second vial and poured its contents into the cup.

Bolan had seen this newly developed serum only once before. The chemical was rapidly absorbed through the skin, but was most effective when administered orally. In less than thirty seconds, Brother Thomas visibly relaxed.

"Drink this, please," Dr. Lacey said, handing him the cup.

When Thomas did as he was told, Bolan knew the drug was already working.

"I'll be downstairs," Lacey said, pulling off his gloves while walking to the door. "The next thirty minutes will be very good. After that, it starts to degrade."

Bolan turned immediately to Thomas and asked, "Where are the Forty Martyrs?"

Thomas answered as if having a conversation with an old friend. His eyes were alert and sharp, and his speech showed no signs of slurring. The wonder of the drug was that it produced absolutely no physical symptoms.

"In the United States," Thomas replied right away.

"Where in the United States?"

Thomas shook his head and answered, "Somewhere close to Boston. I don't know where."

"Is the disease complete?" Bolan asked.

"Not yet. I don't think so."

"When did MacPherson finish his portion?"

"Last week." His eyes wandered about the room, coming back to rest on Bolan.

"Where is his part now?"

"We sent it to Bermuda."

"How?"

"We sent the package by airplane."

"When?"

"Yesterday."

Through his cell phone on the chair, Bolan heard Price shouting to Kurtzman that the plane left Australia yesterday. He paused for a second to think about phrasing his next question. It was important that he not plant ideas in the Order member's head.

Remembering something LaFontaine had said in the Royal Botanic Gardens, Bolan asked, "Why didn't you hide MacPherson's body? Did you want him to be found by the police?"

"Blessed are they who die in the service of the Lord, that they may rest from their labors. For their deeds follow them. Dr. MacPherson deserved a proper burial."

"Where will the final disease be assembled?"

Thomas looked down into his lap and replied, "Boston."

"Who will assemble the final disease?"

"Abbot Gabriel," he replied as if the answer was obvious.

"Where is Abbot Gabriel now?"

"He's in Boston."

"Do you know where?" Bolan asked.

"No. I don't know."

Bolan checked his watch. He had reached the first dead end. Thomas gazed at him, a serene look on his face.

"Ask him about the antidote," Price's voice said from the cell phone.

"Who's that?" Thomas asked, stretching his neck to look beyond Bolan as if he thought someone might be lying on the floor next to the bed.

"One of our friends," Bolan answered, his words eliciting a short, agreeable nod from his prisoner. "Is there an antidote?"

"Yes, there is."

"Where is it?"

"I don't know that."

"When will the disease be released?"

"When God tells Abbot Gabriel that the time is right."

"Does Abbot Gabriel receive visions from God?" Bolan continued.

"Yes. Abbot Gabriel saw you when you traveled to Boston. Abbot Gabriel saw you coming to Australia." He paused for a few seconds before adding, "Yes, he gets visions from God."

"When did he start getting the visions?"

Thomas shrugged. "When the previous Abbot Gabriel died."

"The previous abbot was also named Gabriel?"

"All our abbots are Gabriel."

"What was Abbot Gabriel's name before he became abbot?" Bolan asked.

"He was Brother Timothy," Thomas replied.

"What was his last name?"

"I don't know. Last names are material. They have no place in the service of the Lord."

Price broke in again. "Ask him about their facility."

"How many brothers are at your site outside Sydney?"

"Sixteen of the faithful are there."

"What kind of weapons do you have?"

He looked dead at Bolan and said, "The soldier of the Beast is coming. But an American machine gun will stop the forces of the Beast on consecrated ground. And the Lord will smite our enemies."

"Ask him about the lab," Price said.

"Where in the building is the lab?"

"It's not. We converted the chapel into a work space for Dr. MacPherson's holy work."

"Is the lab still operational?" Bolan asked.

"I don't know. I haven't been inside for a while. My service to the Lord did not require that I had contact with Dr. MacPherson."

Bolan looked at his watch, saw it was getting close to four o'clock. The drug would soon begin degrading. He spoke into the phone. "Anything else?"

"No. It'll be dark there soon. I'm calling LaFontaine. Get out to their place and secure the lab!" Price said.

"Wilco," Bolan replied, but he sensed they were already too late.

14

With the short days winter brought to Australia, it was pitch black by the time LaFontaine and Bolan reached a deserted spot almost two hours north of Sydney. The field agent pulled his Ford SUV into the woods off the paved highway and sat for a moment, breathing rapidly.

"You're sure this is the place?" Bolan asked.

"Half a mile straight through these woods," LaFontaine said. "I've been here three times already. Don't worry. I know exactly where we are."

They were dressed entirely in black, with face paint already applied to dull any shine or reflection. LaFontaine had brought web belts, white phosphorous flares, smoke canisters, and the ten box magazines for their Spectre submachine guns he had reloaded to mix tracers in with the ball ammunition. The night-vision goggles they were using for this mission included red lenses. When the goggles were turned off, Bolan and LaFontaine could use them to see in the harsh white light of the flares without degrading their natural night vision.

"We have to take the lab intact," Bolan said as they stood outside the SUV and pulled on their web gear.

"Got it," LaFontaine replied lightly.

Bolan reached over and grabbed LaFontaine by the front

of his shirt. "Listen to me," he said in a threatening voice, pulling the agent so close he could smell the sickly sweet smell of the adrenaline-laced sweat already breaking out on his partner's brow. "Intact means no damage. The lab is a separate building. If you damage it in any way, I'll have your ass shipped out to Antarctica."

"I said I got it," LaFontaine answered, pushing Bolan's hand away.

"Okay. The one I questioned said they have an American machine gun. It's probably an M-60, and if they know what they're doing, they'll have it set for grazing fire. They know we're coming."

Bolan knew for nighttime defenses, the standard ammo mix was four M-80 ball cartridges followed by one M-62 tracer. Grazing fire was set when the guns were calibrated to shoot no higher than knee level, sending a wall of lead approximately eighteen inches above ground in front of the entire position. It was an extremely effective tactic to prevent an overrun.

"The ammo's 7.62?" LaFontaine asked as he finished his final preparations and attached the comm unit to his ear.

"Yeah. And if it came from an American unit, we won't be the only ones using tracers," Bolan said.

"Rock and roll!" LaFontaine said.

"Just remember what I told you about the lab."

Without answering, the agent set off through the woods with Bolan right behind.

"What about booby traps?" the soldier asked softly, knowing his jaw mike would amplify his voice.

"No." LaFontaine came loud and clear through his earpiece. "I was here this afternoon when you were at the house with Hannigan. We have a clean approach all the way to an open field right next to their compound. Two buildings, fifty yards in between. The main place and your freakin' precious lab. There's a position fortified with sandbags against the southeast corner of the house. That's where the gun must be. It's facing the field we're coming into."

"Were you going to tell me this ahead of time?" Bolan asked angrily.

"I just did," LaFontaine said.

The Australian countryside was dark under a moonless winter sky. Bolan and LaFontaine donned and adjusted their night-vision goggles as they walked, which, because of the red lenses, were not quite as effective as they would normally be. It was a small price to pay, however, for being able to use white phosphorous flares, another element Bolan knew induced terror in an enemy. The stark brilliant light would turn a dark landscape into a surrealistic two-dimensional, high-contrast kill zone where everything was either black or white. The flares burned out abruptly instead of tapering off and growing dim like a lantern running out of fuel or a flashlight with a dying battery. All at once the enemy was plunged from center-stage glare into total darkness. If they didn't know how to preserve their visual purple, they'd be night blind for minutes afterward, as if someone had taken their picture with a flash bulb.

Infantry officers drilled their troops to immediately react and hit the ground as soon as the characteristic pop of a flare was heard. The officers and noncoms knew that even when their soldiers received the proper training, a combination of flares and tracers along with rapid alternating between intense light and total blackness were conditions perfect for fostering unrestrained panic. Hugging the ground with eyes closed until a flare's light went out not only reduced the chance of motion drawing an enemy's eye, it also mitigated the fright a rookie soldier would experience.

The Australian underbrush was sparse, allowing Bolan and LaFontaine to move quickly through the trees. The terrain in the area was a little bumpy, creating depressions and swells large enough for a person to find cover, a fact Bolan tucked into the back of his brain. It took them slightly less than fifteen minutes to reach the edge of the coppice, where they split twenty yards apart before both dropping to one knee. In the greenish glow produced by the goggles, they surveyed the buildings directly across the rolling field covered with ankle-deep grass.

"Can you see the gun position?" LaFontaine asked.

"Yeah. It's well-placed. If we didn't know to be looking for it, we may have been halfway across the field before realizing it was there."

"How many men do you think we're up against?"

"The prisoner we took said sixteen, but I don't know if that included him and the other two."

"Thirteen, sixteen, same difference," LaFontaine said.

"Okay," Bolan said into his mike, "we don't want a frontal attack. Let's get as far to the sides as we can, find a depression to get low, and we'll pop some flares. Make sure you keep your goggles on. They won't know where the flares are coming from, and they'll probably react by firing across the entire front. So stay low. The M-60 muzzle-blast should give us a good look at the gun position. As soon as the flares go out, hit with a full magazine from the Spectre. Taking out the gun is our first objective."

"I've done this before," LaFontaine said with an irritated edge to his voice.

"Me too. I don't want it to be our last. Let's go. Keep in touch."

"Wilco," LaFontaine said in an excited whisper as they

began moving into position. Through his earpiece, Bolan could hear the agent's breathing, suddenly quick and raspy as adrenaline surged through his system.

Bolan angled off to the right, the goggles enabling him to keep his enemy in sight. Until the first shot was fired, he and LaFontaine held the upper hand. The enemy might be expecting them, but when soldiers were in a defensive position awaiting an attack they knew was coming, each minute dragged as if it were an hour. Once the firing started, time moved the opposite way, with troops finding after the lead stopped flying that what they thought happened within minutes had actually taken much longer.

"I'm at nine o'clock to the gunner," Bolan said, finding a depression at the edge of the field. "I have a good spot. Tell me when you're ready."

"Not yet," LaFontaine came back.

Bolan touch-checked his gear, making sure the 50-round magazine was locked into the Spectre's ammo port, that the paper seals on the six flares sticking out from one of his web belt pouches were ripped open and that the automatic pistol he carried in its shoulder holster was loaded with the safety off. The pistol was not silenced, as the Executioner wanted as much chaos and noise on the battlefield as possible. The ACP+P .45-caliber ammunition would add one more violent voice to what Bolan hoped would already be an insane cacophony.

As a final check, he ran his left hand over the three M-18 smoke canisters clipped to the belt's suspenders, and the four chunks of C-4 plastique with their blasting caps and detonator in the left front pouch.

"Okay, I'm in place. Two o'clock to the gunner," came through his earpiece.

"Two flares each, no delay," Bolan said. He waited for the few seconds it took to take the top cap containing the firing pin off two of his flare tubes and place them on the tapered bottom where they'd ignite the propellant. "Three… two…one…fire."

Holding the flare in his left hand at a slight angle to send it above the main building, Bolan slapped the bottom of the tube sharply, driving the firing pin into the bottom where the propellant was stored. He immediately felt a whoosh of air as the flare sped skyward. Without pausing, he dropped the spent tube, grabbed the second flare and repeated the slapping action. As soon as it was skyward, he pulled his head below the berm formed by the depression in which he lay.

Ticking off the seconds in his head, Bolan heard the four distinctive pops, coming so close together they were almost simultaneous. LaFontaine had also done a good job launching his flares.

The landscape was suddenly as brightly lit as a Broadway stage under full spotlights as the white phosphorous ignited and the flares drifted slowly toward earth under tiny silk parachutes. The M-60 machine gun opened fire, its eardrum throbbing rat-a-tat echoing through the woods in a steady response to the sudden light. Tracers flew inches above Bolan's face as he hugged the contour of the depression. As he suspected they would, the gun team, comprised of a gunner and an assistant who fed a belt of 7.62 mm ammo into the gun's side port, was sweeping the area to their front from left to right. When Bolan saw the tracers cutting through the trees behind him start to move away from his position toward LaFontaine, he said, "Incoming your way," into his jaw mike while raising his head to peek over the edge of the berm.

The M-60's muzzle-flashes illuminated four men in the gun position behind the sandbags, and at least five or six others were firing wildly from windows in the main building. Two groups of three men each were positioned behind what looked like stacked logs on each side of the main building, apparently thinking they could effectively defend a flanking assault from either direction. All were firing their weapons on full-auto.

Somewhere in the back of Bolan's mind, a clock involuntarily kept time on the burning flares. Having used white phosphorous so often, he instinctively knew the moment they would go out.

As they had done upon igniting, the four flares blinked out within milliseconds of one another, and the suddenly black night was filled with the terror-inducing screams of the Spectre submachine guns. One hundred rounds of 9 mm lead laced with NATO tracers converged onto the gun site from nine o'clock and two o'clock at a mind-numbing rate. The sandbags protecting the gun site appeared to explode under the barrage of steady slugs slamming into the position.

The gunner and his assistant were hit multiple times, their bodies jerking and dancing as the full-jacketed rounds tore their flesh to pieces. The rapid fire quickly exhausted the ammunition in the box magazine, and Bolan pulled back under cover of the berm, the barrel of the Italian gun smoking from the friction its quick work produced.

LaFontaine's gun also fell silent. From the house, gunmen fired toward the spots from which the incoming tracers had originated. With 5.7 mm rounds snapping the air a finger's width above his head, Bolan spoke.

"You okay?"

"Yeah. Nice job. Think we got all four?" LaFontaine asked, referring to the two gun teams behind the sandbags.

"I know we got two. Don't know if the second team kept down. The ones in the house have our locations. Let's move. I'm going to the right, trying to get around seven o'clock," Bolan said.

"I'll move to high noon."

Bolan took off running in a crouch, dashing from one covered spot to another as rounds zipped through the air, some dangerously close, others not so. He moved as if he was in full daylight view, diving for cover, then bringing his legs up under him like coiled springs so he could burst forward en route to a new spot. In a matter of minutes, he reached a point almost directly behind the gun site.

The view through the goggles, reduced in intensity by the red lenses, showed a panicked enemy. The secondary gun team had apparently taken effective cover and kept down throughout the first assault, because they were now in place. Bolan heard the recognizable sound of the M-60's cover slamming down, indicating a fresh belt of ammunition had just been loaded.

The Order's gunmen stopped firing, and silence as deep as the darkness settled over the battlefield.

Suicide troops, Bolan thought. Inexperienced and poorly trained, there was no doubt in his mind they would all end up dead.

"I'm in place at seven o'clock," Bolan said into his mike, taking a fresh 50-round box magazine and ramming it home. He slid the Spectre's bolt to the rear and let it fly forward to chamber the first round.

"Not yet," LaFontaine replied. "Second verse same as the first. Hold on."

Bolan prepared his final two flares and placed them on the ground. The silence of the night grew long.

"Okay," LaFontaine said.

As he had for the first volley, Bolan counted them down.

Bolan smacked the first flare's bottom, heard it launch, grabbed the second and repeated his action.

Before they ignited, he pulled the Spectre into place and got ready to peek out from behind the tree he was using for cover. His position was on the edge of the field, less than thirty yards from the main building.

The four flares popped, and once again the countryside was bathed in brilliant harsh light. The M-60 team began hosing the woods with a steady stream of deadly 7.62 mm NATO rounds, the noise deafening. Most of the fire was directed toward the positions Bolan and LaFontaine had vacated, but Bolan maintained his discipline by peering around his cover through the red lenses, marking in his mind where the targets were.

On his side of the house, the three men behind the stacked logs armed with submachine guns had positioned themselves to face toward the side and back, perhaps assuming that the M-60 at the corner of the house would take care of a frontal assault. Men continued to fire sporadically from windows in the house, but there were no targets to be seen, and this time, they did not panic and fire as wildly as they had during Bolan and LaFontaine's first attack.

Bolan readied himself as the flare time ran short, placing his finger on the Spectre's trigger. As soon as the flares went out, he opened fire, sending a hailstorm of tracer-laced slugs first into the gun site, which was also taking a beating from LaFontaine's straight-ahead position. When the M-60 fell silent, Bolan shifted his aim to the three gunmen behind the logs who were directing their fire his way. He finished the magazine, ejected the empty box, and without wasting a second, grabbed the next one from his pouch and shoved it into the submachine gun's ammo port.

Holding the Spectre at waist level, he sprang from behind the cover of the tree and dashed forward, angling his way toward an outcropping, dodging and weaving like a wide receiver in the open field with the goal line in sight. While he ran, he fired the Spectre in short bursts, engaging targets of opportunity as they appeared.

A man swung into view in a second-floor window, a P-90 held to his shoulder, and Bolan hammered him back into the middle of the room with a quick blast of 9 mm lead. Bullets were flying through the air from the three behind the logs, and as Bolan launched himself into a dive that would take him to his intended spot behind the rocks, he felt the sting of a round scratch the top of his scalp. He twisted in midair to direct his reply at the shooter, sending a burst of a dozen slugs into him and the man who knelt nearby.

The first gunman was lifted clean off his feet, his finger frozen in a death grip on the trigger of his P-90, sending a wild spray into the side of the house until the rounds in his magazine were consumed. His partner spun 180 degrees under the force of the bullets, falling dead as Bolan hit the ground behind the rocks.

The smell of burning hair filled his nostrils, taking him a second to realize it was his. He touched the top of his head, and although his hand came away hot and wet, he wasn't light-headed or dizzy, so he knew the wound was nothing more than a scrape. Without looking out from behind the rocks, he fired the remaining rounds from his Spectre in the direction of the building's second-floor windows.

"How're you doing?" he asked into the mike as he grabbed one of his two remaining box magazines to replace the spent one.

"The M-60 is out," LaFontaine shouted back.

"Throw the smoke and give me cover. I have plastique for the four corners. Let's blow this building," Bolan said.

LaFontaine responded immediately to Bolan's direction, tossing two M-18 smoke canisters toward the front of the house. Bolan did the same from approximately twenty yards off the side of the house, and the M-18s blanketed the area in thick rolling clouds of toxic smelling smoke. As the dense swirls filled the air, adding to the confusion and disarray, Bolan watched for the muzzle-flash of the third gunman behind the logs. He saw it simultaneous with a volley that hit the rocks in front of him, whining and pinwheeling with whizzing noises as they ricocheted into space on random tangents. Bolan caressed the trigger of the Italian gun, sending two hot tracers along with their companion rounds into the gut of the gunman, whose final scream as the bullets found their mark tapered off.

Men from the other side of the house appeared at the rear, putting Bolan under fire from his flank. He immediately rolled away from the rocks, firing at the new targets from an exposed position. Keeping his finger on the trigger of his weapon, Bolan drove the three back behind the building with a volley that ended when his bolt clicked open on an empty chamber. Grabbing his final box magazine, he ejected the used one, rammed the new one home and jumped to his feet for a dash to the building's back corner.

"Last box," he said into the mike. "I'm charging the house."

"I'm right behind!" LaFontaine responded.

While running a zigzag pattern across the open space between the rocks and the house, Bolan searched for muzzle-flashes as he fired his Spectre in short staccato statements that contrasted the steady buzz pummeling the building's second floor from LaFontaine's weapon. A muzzle-flash winked through the smoke off to his left, and Bolan engaged it immediately, knowing he had hit the source when the gun fired out of control as the owner fell to the ground. Upon reaching the back corner of the house, he dived for the ground and peeked at ground level along the back wall.

The three men he had driven away were at the far end of the building in a similar position to his, and they opened fire as soon as Bolan poked his head around the corner. He drew back as a flurry of bullets chewed up the earth where his face had been a moment before.

With his back pressed against the wall, he reached into his front pouch, grabbed a chunk of C-4 plastique and jammed it into the seam where the building's first floor rested on its stone and foundation. The substance filled the wide crack as he forced it inward, sticking one of the blasting caps into the gray blob.

"Three gunmen out back," he said. "Flank 'em left. I'm coming to the M-60."

"Wilco," LaFontaine replied, and the stream of bullets flying into the second floor windows ceased.

Bolan rushed along the side of the building, alert for movement in the smoke. A man ran from the front of the house toward the rear, passing so close to Bolan they could have reached out and slapped a high five as he went by. Too late, he realized Bolan was not one of the Order, and attempted to spin the barrel of his P-90 around in order to engage him. Before he could do so, Bolan loosed a barrage at almost point-blank range. At such close proximity, the 9 mm Parabellum rounds almost cut the man in two, doubling him over as he was sent flying toward the rear of the house. His corpse bounced once before coming to rest in a tattered heap close to the spot he was originally attempting to reach.

"I'm at the M-60," Bolan said when he reached the corner of the building where the gun site was set. Four bodies lay in grotesque death poses, their limbs twisted in ways they had never assumed while alive.

Without wasting any time, Bolan reached into his pouch, grabbed another piece of C-4 and jammed it into the crack between foundation and floor. As he was ramming the blasting cap into the explosive, a shooter on the second floor stuck the barrel of his P-90 out the window and began firing.

Bolan threw himself away from the building, landing on his back behind the chewed-up sandbags positioned around the idle machine gun. Looking straight up, he let loose with the Spectre, the rapid rate of fire sending a stream of bullets into the gunman's exposed weapon and hand. The rifle shattered upon impact with the bullets, falling to the ground along with what looked to Bolan to be most of the gunner's hand.

"Coming across the front. Where are you?" Bolan said into this mike.

"Corner where you're heading," LaFontaine replied as the uniquely chaotic sounds of a close-in firefight reached Bolan's ears from every direction. As he ran in front of the house, he fired his Spectre in short bursts, aiming at muzzle-flashes visible through the smoke. The enemy had been greatly thinned, with perhaps only four or five remaining.

Bolan dropped the empty Spectre and drew his Mk.23

pistol from its shoulder holster as he reached the building's front left corner. LaFontaine was in a kneeling position out in the open, hosing the side of the house with a steady stream from his gun.

"Hurry!" he said. "This is my last box."

Bolan ran to the corner, taking a quick glance behind him as he reached his destination. A gunman with P-90 blazing burst from the opening where the front door had been, tripping over the wooden remnants that littered the threshold. With well-honed reflexes Bolan fired the Mk.23 with his right hand while reaching into his pouch and grabbing a charge of C-4 with his left. The hefty .45-caliber bullet caught the stumbling man in the neck before he could recover from his missed footing, releasing a crimson fountain.

Bolan quickly placed the explosive in the same manner he had set the others, noticing from the corner of his eye that LaFontaine had also discarded his Spectre and was firing his SIG-Sauer as fast as he could pull the trigger.

LaFontaine's cover did the trick, allowing Bolan to shove the blasting cap into the wad of C-4.

"Back corner. Let's go," Bolan said, and they took off running along the side of the house, their handguns sending a wall of Parabellum lead to cover the way to their destination. From the woods behind the house, three P-90s chattering in their 5.7 mm pitch took them under fire, and Bolan and LaFontaine dived to the ground together, answering rapidly with their pistols. A medley of painful shrieks indicated their rounds had at least wounded their enemies.

LaFontaine ejected a magazine and rammed a fresh one home, his hands moving in a blur. As he resumed shooting into the woods at what was the only threat at that moment, Bolan scrambled the rest of the way to the final corner of the house to place his remaining C-4. The instant he shoved the blasting cap into the explosive, two men from above engaged his position. Clods of earth jumped and danced at his feet as he pressed himself against the side of the house, unable to get a good angle to return fire.

"Above me," he said into the mike.

LaFontaine's SIG-Sauer roared in response, driving the men away from the window.

"Fire in the hole," Bolan said, running forward into the woods behind the house. There was movement in the brush to the front, and both Bolan and LaFontaine let loose with volleys from their handguns, the 9 mm and .45-caliber rounds singing a song of death in close two-part harmony.

Their eyes searching through the bushes and trees for surviving gunmen, Bolan and LaFontaine continued sprinting through the woods until they were roughly fifty yards from the house. When Bolan dived behind a clump of trees, LaFontaine followed his example, knowing the time for detonation had arrived.

Bolan reached into his pouch, his fingers closing around the remote detonator. With his thumb, he depressed the lever, slid it in its channel from the unit's front to rear and depressed the trigger.

The C-4 charges exploded with a flash that shot a column of orange fire two hundred feet into the air. A shock wave raced through the woods, snapping branches off trees while bending saplings to the ground. The accompanying blast pounded Bolan's eardrums a nanosecond later, producing a buzz similar to that felt when a bolt of lightning strikes the ground within feet of someone caught out in the open.

"Holy freakin' shit!" LaFontaine said into Bolan's ringing ear as the entire building burst into flames as it crashed to the earth.

The two lay motionless for a few minutes while the fire raced through the wood frame structure, engulfing it entirely within seconds.

Making sure their weapons held fresh magazines, Bolan and LaFontaine rose and began moving back toward the battlefield. Reaching the edge of the woods with no sign of the enemy, they stayed close to the tree line as they made their way cautiously toward the chapel.

By the time they reached the building that had been converted into MacPherson's laboratory, they were convinced there was no remaining resistance. But for one surviving prisoner, the last remnants of the Order of Raphael had been eliminated from the Australian continent.

The battle down under was over, and Bolan's mind shifted to the remaining challenge. He threw open the door to the chapel, finding a completely empty space. The Order had apparently been planning to desert this site as they had Boston and Bayonne. A war with millions of lives at stake loomed on the horizon ten thousand miles away.

As he and LaFontaine walked slowly through the woods toward the spot where their SUV was parked, Bolan pondered the current situation. A disease with the potential to end humankind was progressing through its birth canal, its evil midwives readying themselves for delivery somewhere in Boston. He prayed that Kurtzman's team at Stony Man Farm had made a breakthrough, realizing that if they did not find Gabriel before he assembled the disease's three components, the first of the Forty Martyrs might soon be dispatched.

When they reached the car, he pulled his cell phone from

the glove compartment and speed-dialed Barbara Price's number to report that the site formally occupied by the Order of Raphael was now ready to be cleaned.

15

When Bolan entered the Computer Room at Stony Man Farm, his nostrils were accosted by a faintly pleasant smell.

The team had been working for two days straight, catching sleep in one-hour snatches only when their fingers cramped or their minds shut down out of exhaustion. Despite the climate-controlled environment that kept the temperature and humidity at computer-friendly levels, the air held a pungent aroma composed of electrical ozone, pizza sauce and burned coffee. Barbara Price glanced up as Bolan entered, her puffy eyes staring at him.

"Good job down under," she said.

"LaFontaine is a loose cannon."

"That's why he's on the Australian continent," Price said with a laugh.

Brognola's voice came over a speakerphone placed in an open spot on Kurtzman's work surface.

"I'm back. Where are we?" he asked the team, and Bolan realized they were keeping an open line for the big Fed to remain updated while he completed other duties that probably included briefing the President at least hourly.

"Bear is on a short break," Price answered. "Carmen is searching for the ship, everyone else is still sifting through tons of airport data trying to find hands with scars. The systems for airport security unfortunately are programmed for face recognition, forcing the team to manually scan billions of files looking for marks on passengers' left hands. No one—" Price began to say when she was interrupted.

"I think I have the ship," Delahunt yelled from across the room, where she was typing on the keyboard with her left hand while rolling and depressing a trackball mounted next to the text keys with her right.

Tokaido glanced over his shoulder toward Delahunt for a moment, his head moving in time to the rock music from his ever-present earbuds. Bolan had noticed from working with him that a good measure of the hacker's stress level was reflected in the speed with which he chewed and snapped his bubble gum. This day, he was chewing and moving the wad around the inside of his mouth as if his tongue was in a contest with his fingers to see which could move faster.

Wethers also looked up from his keyboard for a second to nod at Delahunt before burying his face back in his work.

Bolan walked over to Delahunt's station as she pulled and sorted data. Each of her three monitors showed a slightly different version of an overlay displaying a portion of the Atlantic Ocean from Bermuda to Boston.

Hundreds of multicolored dots and triangles representing individual crafts covered the screens, moving at a snail's pace in all directions. The combination of color and shape represented what Delahunt called the degree of reality.

Some vessels were being displayed real time, tracked by the government's Global Precise Positioning Service via twenty-four satellites deployed twelve thousand miles high at an angle of fifty-five degrees to the equator. Others were time delayed, the result of complicated algorithms and regression analyses employed when they drifted into areas temporarily outside the GPPS coverage. Some were completely virtual, using a combination of source data from multiple systems to display where certain ships, having already arrived at their destination, had traveled over the previous thirty-six hours. Data on all vessels, whether they be real time, time delayed, or virtual, were subjected to numerous computer analyses using smart programs to investigate factors ranging from owner profiles to previous course history. The mountain of information being gathered was intended to narrow the funnel, enabling the cybernetics team's search to zero in and identify a single ship.

In the left top section of Delahunt's center console, one of the triangles was blinking, indicating it had successfully been filtered through all the criteria established by their integrated programs and algorithms.

Kurtzman came back into the room, the door closing behind his wheelchair. He pushed himself directly to Delahunt's station and stared at her screen while she pointed at it.

"Yesterday. The *Titan*."

She rolled the trackball, and a ship's manifest jumped into the center of her right screen. "Registered in Brazil," she said loud enough for everyone including Brognola to hear, "stopover in Hamilton, Bermuda. Trade vessel bringing finished goods, mostly running shoes and clothes, into Boston." She rolled and depressed the trackball, and the manifest flipped from page to page. "I'm looking at what was loaded in Hamilton. More clothes, golfing supplies, sails and three cases of wine marked for pickup at the docks in Boston by Great White Importers. And one passenger also got on in Hamilton. That's odd, isn't it? For a trade ship to take on a passenger? Ernesto Gracho."

"Spelling?" Kurtzman asked, his computer already open to links with U.S. Customs and Immigration.

"You said yesterday?" Kurtzman asked.

"The ship arrived yesterday in Boston," Delahunt said.

Brognola's voice came over the phone. "I'm talking on the other line to Great White Importers. They don't know anything about a shipment of wine from Bermuda. They say they haven't brought anything into Boston for more than a week."

"Immigration confirms Gracho," Kurtzman said from his workstation. "I'm on instant message with a contact." He paused, typed a few sentences in rapid fire, then said, "Gracho had Jamaican papers. He gave Immigration a Boston address where he's supposedly visiting an aunt." He paused while another line appeared on instant messenger. "He acted as the importing agent to bring the wine through customs."

Kurtzman pressed a key and a printed page leaped from the high-speed laser printer next to his workstation. He pushed his chair back a few inches, reached over and grabbed the output.

"Is Striker there?" Brognola asked.

"I am."

"The chopper can get you to Boston in under two hours. Go up there and get Gracho."

Bolan took the proffered printed page from Kurtzman's hand and quickly left the Computer Room. On his way to the helicopter pad, he swung by his quarters to get his Beretta 93-R.

HAL BROGNOLA'S FRUSTRATION came through the speakerphone in Stony Man Farm's Computer Room. It was a three-way telecom, linking the big Fed with Barbara Price and Mack Bolan.

"Read the address again," he directed, and Bolan read into his cell phone what was printed on the paper he had taken from Kurtzman.

"Yeah. That's what he gave Immigration and Customs," Price said. "You're sure you're on the right street?"

Bolan looked again at the street sign on the telephone pole in front of him, then at the number on the door of the coffee shop, and said, "Gracho must be a member in the Order. The address he gave is valid, I'm sure I'm in the right place and it's not a residence. It's a coffee and doughnut shop."

He told them what he thought about the Order's choice to transport the bioweapon in wine bottles, receiving immediate agreement from Kurtzman.

"Good insight, Striker," Kurtzman said into the speaker. "That's their core competency. Not that it does us any good. We're still plowing our way through the airport data."

"While I'm up here, I'll swing by the docks and see if I can speak to the crew who unloaded the ship. Maybe one of them talked to Gracho."

"Good idea," Brognola answered with a sigh indicating that he, like everyone else, was approaching his point of mental exhaustion.

INDUSTRIAL RECEIVING DOCKS, as well as the companies and people who both frequent and support them, were similar in every corner of the globe, Bolan thought. The loading docks themselves, worked by members of the longshoreman's union, were akin to the deck of an aircraft carrier in terms of activity and potential danger. Multiton forklifts sped up and down ramps unloading pallets, while overhead cranes lifted sea containers from the decks and holds of ships, placing them directly onto flatbeds transporting them to short-term warehouses.

The environment was a rough place for rough people.

The approach leading to Boston's industrial docks was down a two-lane street through a section of gritty bars and flophouses where men who had been at sea for extended periods could satisfy their pent-up needs. As the Executioner neared a one-story, flat-roofed wooden establishment looking more like a trailer than a bar, sounds of angry voices drifted into the street from the open door. There were no sidewalks. A gutter littered with cigarette butts and miscellaneous trash extended from the bar's door ten feet or so to the street's asphalt. As Bolan passed, he glanced inside, but with the only apparent light coming from neon swirls spelling out various beer brands, he couldn't see much.

Two shiny Harley-Davidson motorcycles were parked in the gutter to one side of the door, their low seats and curving lines suggestive of power and speed.

"The fuck you looking at?" came from a far corner of the run-down building where two overweight men sat against the foundation sharing a reefer. They were dressed in jeans and denim vests over white T-shirts, looking more than a bit like inmates. One wore a heavy chrome chain around his chest and right shoulder the way Bolan had at times humped belts of ammunition across jungle trails. The Executioner walked quickly past, intent on reaching the docks.

When Bolan got to the wharf, he was surprised to see the *Titan* tied up, taking on cargo. He had thought she would have been gone by now. She was small for an oceangoing transport, no more than a hundred feet long. She was painted red above black, the shallowness of her draw indicating her cargo compartments were nowhere close to being full. Forklifts were bringing loads of computer software up a wide loading ramp, the stacked cartons held together by shrink-wrap plastic that sparkled in the sunshine.

A man wearing a long sleeved black shirt with the ship's name stitched in white block letters on the breast pocket was leaning against the gangplank, smoking a cigarette.

"Hi, there," Bolan said, approaching. "Is the captain around?"

"We ain't taking on no new crew," the man answered, eyeing Bolan from top to bottom. "You look like you could handle yourself, though."

"Not here for a job," Bolan answered. "Just want to talk to the captain for a minute."

The man flicked the butt of his cigarette into the water between the dock and the ship and said, "That's me."

"I need information about a shipment you brought in yesterday."

"Who you working for?"

"Private concern. I don't want to cause you any trouble. The three cases of wine you picked up in Hamilton? And the passenger?"

The captain's eyes narrowed and he asked, "You government?"

Bolan remained silent.

"You the Mob?"

"I don't want to cause you any trouble," Bolan repeated with a steady stare.

"Jesus," the captain said between clenched teeth. "I knew he was bad news. Okay." He took a step closer, his eyes darting around the dock as if he and Bolan were conspirators. "Week ago, we're posting from Panama, I get a call on my cell from someone says his name is Raoul. No last name, just Raoul. I say, 'How'd you get this number?' and he laughs, like we're mates. He knows my itinerary, and tells me I can get two grand for giving a guy a lift from Hamilton to Boston. I think, what the hell? I'm going that way, why not take the money? The guy shows up in Bermuda, says Raoul sent him, and he's bringing three cases of wine. Doesn't want nothing on the manifest, but I'm thinking two grand ain't near enough for smuggling, so I tell him you go on the manifest or you go back to Raoul. He's pissed, but I guess he figures he has no choice. I make him give me the money before he sets one foot on deck, and I give him a lift up here. Everything on the manifest, all proper, I ain't done nothing wrong."

Bolan nodded. "Nothing wrong with that. What can you tell me about him?" he said.

The captain pursed his lips and gave his head a shake. "Only with us one day and night. Gave him an empty berth, he never came out. Kept all the wine with him, so's I'm still thinking smuggling, but it ain't no skin off me. I figure he gets caught in customs, I just tell them what I'm telling you. Funny mark on his hand. At first I think it's a tattoo, but when he's getting off I get a good look. Kind of like a burn or something. Later on? I see him coming out of customs with the wine, and there's three guys waiting for him. I'm up on deck, but I have my glass, so I check them out, and they all have a mark on their hands too. Good riddance, y'know? Who knows what that's all about?"

The captain reached into his shirt pocket, took out a soft pack of Marlboros and shook one loose. He lit it with a disposable lighter. He cupped the flame from the breeze with both hands and repeated, "Good riddance to that shit."

"Did they drive away in a car?" Bolan asked.

"Did they ever. One of them big Porsche SUVs. Getting a Porsche, who picks the SUV? What's with that? Why do they even make them?" He shook his head, sniffed and flicked ashes off the end of his cigarette.

"Did you see the license plate?"

"I told you I had my glass. Rhode Island. Don't remember the number, though."

Bolan thanked the captain and left, pulling out his cell phone as he walked away.

Barbara Price answered her line.

"Gracho had the scar. So did three guys who picked him up in a Porsche SUV. Rhode Island plates. I'm on my way back," Bolan said.

"Thanks," she replied, and the line went dead.

As Bolan walked back the way he had come in, he could picture the team jumping on the new information, with Akira Tokaido immediately hacking into the Rhode Island Division of Motor Vehicles in order to find every Porsche SUV registered in the state. The only question was, would they be able to find it before Brother Gabriel was able to have his man in Boston recreate Dr. Zagorski's work?

Bolan saw the two motorcycle guys get up and walk to the edge of the street when he was still fifty yards away. As he approached, he considered his options. He could cross to the far side of the street, he could draw his Beretta, or he could ignore them and walk straight by as if they weren't there.

He chose the third, but as he drew close, they stepped into the street, and the one with the chain took it off his shoulder and held it by his side.

"My business isn't your business," Bolan said when he was close enough to be heard.

They rushed forward without uttering a single word, the one with the chain bringing his hand up over his shoulder the way a pitcher threw a fastball. Bolan dodged the chain as it came slicing through the air and took a step into his attackers. Rotating his shoulders clockwise, he shot his left arm forward, driving two stiff fingers into the man's armpit while extending his right hand to the rear.

The struck man froze for a second as if an electric current was passing through his body before he howled and dropped the chain. Bolan twisted the other way, withdrawing his left hand while driving his right one forward, smashing its heel into the other man's face. Concurrent with the crunching sound of a nose breaking, a torrent of blood poured forth onto the front of his open vest, turning the white shirt underneath a bright red.

Letting his momentum carry him forward, Bolan planted his left foot while rotating his hips. His right leg shot into the air as he bent at the waist, hitting the chain swinger under the chin with the front of his foot. The man's head jerked back so sharply Bolan thought he heard his neck snap. Despite the aerodynamic constraints of a huge gut hanging over his belt, the man left his feet, coming down unconscious on the parked Harleys. They crashed to the ground, the first pushing over the one next to it.

Bolan heard the click of a switchblade and turned to face his opponent. The man was breathing hard, having a difficult time due to the blood from his nose getting into his airway. He jabbed the air with his blade, muttering obscenities through clenched teeth.

Bolan launched a short kick from his knee, hitting the biker's wrist sharply enough to send the knife flying. Before his opponent could produce another weapon, Bolan rushed forward, jabbing with both hands. A chop to the throat crunched the man's windpipe an instant before Bolan's elbow exploded into the side of his head, driving him to his knees where he tottered for a second before falling face-first into the gutter.

As Bolan walked away, he pulled his cell phone from his pocket and speed-dialed the number of the helicopter pilot waiting for him across the river.

16

Bolan was across the Computer Room from Hunt Wethers and Akira Tokaido when they experienced their moment of discovery.

"Finally!" Tokaido shouted, throwing his hands above his head in the manner of a prizefighter upon hearing a winning decision. Kurtzman wheeled his chair to sit alongside the duo. The others turned in their swivel chairs and waited for Tokaido to share his victory.

"Remember you asked me to check out his guy Cafard?" he asked no one in particular. "I ran into trouble closing a lead," he said, continuing before anyone answered his question. "Last year, Cafard was an organ donor. Gave a kidney."

"That was hard for you to trace down?" Delahunt asked sarcastically.

The hacker gave her a stare that spoke volumes while he spit a wad of bubble gum into the trash can next to his workstation. With a slight smile touching the corners of his eyes, he reached into his pocket, pulled out a half-wrapped bar of bubble gum and bit off three sections. Pushing them to one side of his mouth where they'd soften up, he said, "The recipient was hard to find. Where he is now, I mean."

"Most likely a blood relative?" Delahunt asked, obviously intrigued at the puzzle unfolding before them. As was her nature, she was trying to anticipate where this information was leading.

Tokaido's mouth was busy chewing the stiff gum into a workable piece, so Wethers answered for him.

"That's what we thought, too. So Tokaido went searching for Cafard's brother. We know he has one—we have the birth records and all that—so we were thinking there would be a record somewhere with his brother's name showing he was the one who got the kidney. No luck. The brother had simply vanished."

"No other siblings?" Delahunt asked, continuing to sift through photo after photo from Boston and New York airport files, calling each one up, glancing for a few seconds, then moving on to the next.

"No," Wethers answered after glancing at Tokaido and getting a nod to continue while the hacker worked his gum. "Robert Cafard and his brother were born in Iran to well-educated parents who were successful members of Tehran's Christian community. Long family history living side by side with Islam, some uncles and aunts in Iran, some in Lebanon." Not being able to resist the college professor in him, he added as an afterthought, "Americans don't understand what a sophisticated country Iran is. Persia has a rich history of tolerance and progress predating the *Mayflower* by centuries."

Tokaido snapped his gum twice in rapid succession and said, "War breaks out all over the region, so the parents immigrated to France when the boys were still young. I traced all four through French customs. I even have photos of them."

Looking straight at Bolan, he asked, "Know what the brother's name was back then?"

"Timothy," he said.

Tokaido smiled. He hit a key on his workstation, and his monitor went blank for a moment before being replaced by a picture of a grieving family at a funeral. Two caskets were being lowered into the ground in front of seven or eight mourners, among them Robert Cafard and a man who bore a strong enough resemblance that people might assume they were brothers.

Tokaido spun and depressed his trackball, and the computer zoomed in on the man next to Cafard. First the face loomed large, then the neck and shoulders as he inched the focus downward until all that filled the screen was an image of the mourner's left hand.

"Abbot Gabriel," Wethers said. "We didn't make the link until Striker's prisoner told him the Order's Abbots always took Gabriel for their name, and that prior to being elected, this one was Timothy."

From across the room, Bolan said, "That's how they knew I was coming. It wasn't a leak from that reporter I met with. It wasn't a vision from God. It was Cafard passing on what Brognola was telling him."

"Bastard!" Brognola's voice came over the speakerphone, and the team realized he had joined them at some point during the presentation.

"Motivation?" Kurtzman asked challengingly. Despite the doomsday scenarios his team was often shouldered to mitigate, he thought it was good for people like Tokaido to be challenged. It made his entire organization stronger when they ran into a brick wall, albeit at that moment, Kurtzman would have given anything for a quick breakthrough to prevent the horrific pandemic looming close on the horizon.

"That double funeral put them both over the top," Wethers replied as Tokaido zoomed out to give a full picture again. "Mother and father visited one of Cafard's uncles in Lebanon. While there, they were both killed by a cluster bomb."

"The United States is the only country that provided cluster bombs to Israel," Delahunt said. "That's why the Forty Martyrs are here. The disease will be contained to North America. Dr. Hannigan said they already have an antidote. That will keep it from spreading."

"Are you saying Sentinelles has the antidote?" Brognola asked over the phone.

"Not yet, I wouldn't think," Wethers replied. "Consider how this will play out. The killer disease spreads like wildfire through the United States, killing between seventy and ninety percent of our population. The rest of the world is terrified. Researchers everywhere are searching for the cure." He paused for dramatic effect before saying theatrically, "And out of France, the country that opposed the now dying United States so often in the Middle East, comes humankind's salvation. A doctor in Sentinelles—an organization dedicated to stop the suffering of children around the world—produces the antidote, and the world moves on without America, the once wealthy country that Sentinelles publicly chastised for not contributing more to its cause."

Tokaido spun and depressed the trackball again, and Abbot Gabriel's face filled the screen.

Bolan concentrated on the image, knowing that when he saw it in person, it would be framed within the sights of either his Desert Eagle or Beretta 93-R.

Delahunt immediately rewrote her search criteria, and her workstation stopped displaying a hand. The individual faces flashing for a microsecond on the screens merged to a blur, and the woman turned away, awaiting the computer's signal that a match had been found.

"He must be taking antirejection drugs," Delahunt said.

"Right," Wethers answered while walking back to his workstation. "For the rest of his life. All transplant recipients do. The body never fully accepts a new organ." He turned and ticked off the names of a number of medications. "They're the most common. I'll start with those."

An alarm went off on Delahunt's computer, and she shouted, "I have a match."

Kurtzman and Bolan went to her station while she retrieved the source video. "American Eagle flight 945 from LaGuardia to T. F. Green airport four days ago. Providence, Rhode Island," she said as the tape played, showing Abbot Gabriel walking through the airport's wide corridor behind security on his way to escalators taking him one level below to street level.

"Connecting flight?" Bolan asked.

"Yes," Delahunt answered, having initiated a backtrace as soon as the flight number was identified. "It's a commuter hop. He's the only one on that flight making a connection out of Europe. Zurich to New York to Providence. Traveling under the name Gabriel Patmos."

"Patmos?" Kurtzman asked.

"An island in the Mediterranean," Bolan said, and then to everyone's surprise, he added, "It's where St. John wrote *Revelation*."

Delahunt had been gathering information on the airport as she researched the flight. "It's a commuter airport. Two hours by car from Boston, he probably wanted to avoid Logan where the 9/11 hijackers took the planes. You'd figure security might be tighter there than anyplace else, just making sure it won't happen again."

"Also," Price said, "Striker told us it was a car with Rhode Island plates that met Gracho and the wine. Abbot Gabriel may have visited the Forty Martyrs before going up to Boston."

"Why do we think he's in Boston?" Brognola's voice asked over the speakerphone.

"Because that's what Striker's prisoner told us," Price answered. "If he has someone recreating Zagorski's work, there are more labs in Boston than there are in Rhode Island. The Order may have created the Boston portion at a site that's still operational."

"And," Wethers said in his deep voice that resonated through the Computer Room, "new prescriptions for anti-rejection meds were sent last week to the CVS on Deerfield Street in Kenmore Square. Patient name Patmos, prescribing physician is Robert Cafard of Sentinelles."

"We need a meeting," Brognola said. "I'll be there in an hour and a half."

17

"I think our course of action is clear," the Executioner said to the other three sitting at the conference table in the War Room at Stony Man Farm. "I'll go to the address Abbot Gabriel provided for his prescriptions and bring him back here. One dose of our truth serum and he'll not only tell us where the Forty Martyrs are, he'll also give us the three pieces of the virus."

"No address," Kurtzman said. "Cell phone number is all the pharmacy has, and they probably got that only because they insist on having some way of getting in touch with people they fill prescriptions for. Especially with a foreign doctor in a foreign country. His prescriptions are set up to be called in for pickup."

"Okay. I'll go up there and take him when he comes to get them."

"We don't know when that will be," Price said.

Turning to Kurtzman, she asked, "Does Hunt have the date the last prescription was filled? He said organ recipients take these drugs daily."

She caught Kurtzman in the middle of gulping a huge mouthful of his potent coffee, and he swallowed it before clearing his throat and answering, "Three days ago, right after he got in-country. These drugs don't keep well. Pharmacies usually dispense them with enough for thirty days at a time. We have no way of knowing how much he brought with him."

"We can't wait," Price said. "I agree with Striker's basic plan. We'll have the pharmacy call the cell number, tell them there's something wrong with the drugs they gave out and that the patient shouldn't take them. They'll say they have a new batch, and they'll stress that it's free, as if that's all they think the customer will be concerned about. Striker will be able to get him when he goes to pick up the new drugs."

"What if he sends someone else to get them?" Kurtzman asked.

"I'll trail whoever picks up the prescriptions. He'll lead me to Gabriel," Bolan said.

"I'll have chase cars waiting in both directions," Brognola said. "How are we coming on finding the car with Rhode Island plates? Can we find them that way?"

"We're lucky it's a small state," Kurtzman said. "We've located and checked out every Porsche Cayenne in Rhode Island except for one. Cash purchase, fake name, fake address in Providence. Real license plates, registered at the dealer. There's an APB out. Akira thinks it's on Aquidneck Island."

In response to Brognola's questioning look, he said, "A strip of land with Newport on one end, Portsmouth on the other, and Middletown in between. Not an island out in the ocean. Connected to the mainland by three bridges. One at each end, one in the middle."

"Why does he think it's there?" Bolan asked.

"Most gas stations have cameras that record license plates

to make sure you don't fill up and just drive away. Tokaido hacked into every station's files in Rhode Island, then created a scatter diagram of where our car showed up. They've topped off the tank a number of times, never at the same place, and the data statistically points straight to Aquidneck Island."

"You said an APB is out?" Bolan asked.

"Yeah," Kurtzman replied. "I don't know if they've stopped using the car, or if the police have just been unlucky. Aquidneck Island isn't small, though, and the APB was only issued yesterday."

Price began drumming the table with her fingers. "We're trying to follow a trail, but you know what we're not doing? We're not looking for clues the way Tokaido kept looking to find out why Cafard's brother Timothy simply vanished when there should have been a record of a Timothy Cafard receiving a transplant." She turned to Bolan and asked, "If you had forty of your combat buddies over to your place for two weeks, what would be different? What should we be looking for that's a direct cause of them being there?"

Kurtzman jumped in and asked, "Do you mean outer signs like what's in the trash? What have neighbors seen and not realized it's out of whack? As I said, Aquidneck Island is not small. We can't go door to door asking if people have noticed a gang of forty monks visiting someone down the street."

Price shook her head. "When I started talking, I wasn't sure what direction I was going, but with your comment about trash, you just made me wonder what these guys eat. Where do they get their food? Not take-out, I bet. It would raise too many eyebrows to go somewhere and buy food for forty every night. How many supermarkets are there on

Aquidneck Island? And do they deliver? That wouldn't be so suspicious. They could call in for basic supplies from a number of supermarkets, have the food delivered on different days. It would be no bigger than a large family's weekly purchase, and they wouldn't be using the SUV to go pick it up."

"Do you think they know we're onto the SUV?" Brognola asked.

"No. There's no reason for them to think we know that. But they may be making an effort to play it safe and lay low as they get closer to reaching their deployment date," Bolan said.

Kurtzman nodded while scratching his chin. "Yeah. I'll ask Akira to hack into the supermarkets' databases and see if there's a pattern over the past two weeks of food purchases big enough to feed a platoon. Nice going."

"You, Striker," Brognola said, "are off to Boston again." Shifting in his chair to face Price, he said, "You're two for two. I say we go with your idea to have the drugstore call and say the drugs were bad. Once we have Abbot Gabriel in hand, we'll decide our next move."

IN ADDITION TO BEING RIGHT in the middle of Boston University's city campus, Kenmore Square was approximately a five-minute walk from Fenway Park. On game nights, students without tickets mobbed the nearby sports bars and restaurants to watch the game and cheer in close proximity to the real thing. After the game, they'd pour into the streets, joining the exiting throngs to either celebrate or commiserate.

From his spot half a mile north of home plate, Bolan could hear the occasional cheers of the sellout crowd when one of their Bosox stuck it to the hated Yankees; and the more frequent moans when the Sox played like a team that could go eighty-six years between winning the World Series. The moans riding the warm summer breeze blowing through Kenmore Square far outnumbered the cheers.

Brognola had come up to Boston earlier that afternoon with Bolan to personally brief the pharmacist. He would have preferred to have one of his men stand in, but was concerned that a new face behind the counter might alert Gabriel to keep on walking instead of picking up his drugs. The pharmacist was sure he'd be able to help the Justice Department conduct its sting against an illicit drug operation. He was a bit puzzled at the drugs involved, but with terrorists these days able to turn MP3 players into detonators, who knew what certain people could do with antirejection chemicals. He called the cell phone number to inform Gabriel Patmos that his drugs were bad, and anytime after seven o'clock he could pick up a new prescription for free.

Sitting on a concrete wall about three feet high that separated the parking lot from that of the pizza parlor next door, Bolan fit right in with the other loiterers hanging around on a warm summer night. He was wearing jeans and his dark blue windbreaker over a gray T-shirt. The Beretta 93-R in the holster on his left shoulder was silenced, and across his stomach, just above his waistband, he wore a Velcro quick-draw pouch containing a tranquilizer pistol.

The tranquilizer belonged to a family of synthetic chemicals designed to mimic the action of compounds produced naturally in the body to control biological variances. The bioregulator substance was a polypeptide chain developed in the late seventies by Soviet scientists specifically to produce a rapid drop in blood pressure. Extremely effective, less

than one microgram induced almost immediate unconsciousness.

People came and went in a steady stream to the drugstore,
each of them falling under the eye of the Executioner. He
had memorized Gabriel's face when it was displayed in the
Computer Room, and was ready to take him in the parking
lot at the very first opportunity. Across the street, he could
see one of Brognola's chase cars parked in a metered spot.

Three kids with BU sweatshirts walked by, grumbling
about the Sox bullpen.

"Game over?" a passing man asked.

"Almost," one of the students answered. "Sox blew it
again."

The cell phone in Bolan's pocket vibrated, a signal from
inside that the man at the pharmacy counter was picking up
Abbot Gabriel's prescriptions. Bolan stood and gazed across
the parking lot into the store. The pharmacist was apologiz-
ing for the bad batch of drugs, using the exact gestures they
had agreed would verify the cell phone's vibration.

The courier was a small man, half Bolan's size, wearing
a yellow-and-green satin jacket that looked more suited for
Latin America or the Caribbean than Kenmore Square.
Bolan recalled that Gracho had come through customs with
Jamaican papers. Seeing him in person, Bolan thought they
may have been genuine.

Gracho exited the drugstore on foot and walked straight
past Bolan's spot while shoving the white paper bag containing a thirty-day supply of two antirejection drugs into the side
pocket of his lightweight jacket. As he passed, Bolan studied him without looking directly his way, getting a good
enough view to realize that he, too, wore a shoulder holster.
Bolan let Gracho cross Deerfield Street into the middle of

Kenmore Square before sliding off the short concrete wall to follow him at a safe distance roughly a block and a half away.

For the first few minutes, Bolan's view of his quarry remained good. He was moving along casually but purposefully, showing no indication he knew he was being followed. The trouble came out of nowhere.

The Red Sox game had just ended, and as Bolan followed about a hundred yards behind Gracho, a crowd of thirty-four thousand frustrated, angry fans poured out of Fenway Park's exits and mobbed the streets with a sea of humanity resembling the start of the New York marathon.

Gracho had reached the pedestrian walkway going above the Mass Pike thirty seconds before the multitude coming north toward Bolan jammed it for people going south. The walkway was approximately two hundred yards long, and as Bolan was held back by a crowd that showed its frustration by shoving and pushing people trying to walk through in the opposite direction, Gracho got farther and farther away. Bolan began throwing the people in front of him out of his path, elbowing against the tide, trying to run to catch up with the courier who had become nothing more than fleeting glimpses of yellow and green in the distance. The Executioner was rapidly losing his target.

Bolan looked up at the ESPN broadcasting blimp hovering over Fenway Park and grabbed his cell phone.

"Yeah, Striker," Tokaido's voice came on, creating an instant image in Bolan's mind of the hacker sitting at his workstation, his earbuds wired into not only the MP3 player but also his cell phone.

"I'm losing my man. Outside Fenway Park. ESPN blimp above." He could hear the keyboard chattering like an

AK-47 on full-auto, and knew the hacker was already miles ahead of what he was about to ask.

"Simulcast on ABC," Tokaido said. "Dedicated feed from the blimp. Line's still open."

"Can you hijack their camera the way you did the screen in the Computer Room? Tell me where a guy in a yellow-and-green jacket going south just across the pedestrian bridge is. Can you do that?"

For several long seconds, all Bolan heard coming over the cell phone was the sound of snapping bubble gum. His other ear was receiving a nonstop load of obscenities and complaints from the people he was trying to push through as he fought the crowd's force.

"Akira, can you do that?" he shouted.

"Look at your cell. That him?"

Bolan took his cell phone from his ear. The tiny two-inch screen displayed a real-time aerial view of the entire pedestrian overpass. As Bolan watched, the camera zoomed in on the south end, picking out a man in a green-and-yellow jacket.

"Yes!" Bolan said, leaning forward to speak without taking his eyes off the screen. "Yes! Stay with him!"

Bolan continued to fight and push his way through the mob, getting farther and farther behind Gracho. On his cell phone screen, he saw his target pass Fenway Park on the left and merge with the exiting fans going south after leaving the game. By the time Bolan finally cleared the pedestrian overpass above the Mass Pike, Gracho had progressed three blocks beyond the stadium, turning right onto Fullerton Street.

As he ran to catch up, Bolan watched Gracho turn into the front walk of a single-family residence six houses down on the right from Brookline. The courier took a few moments unlocking the front door before entering and pulling it closed behind him.

"Got it. Thanks, Akira."

Bolan snapped his cell phone closed, slipped it into his pocket and hustled toward the house where he expected to find Abbot Gabriel.

Fullerton Street was in an old inner-city neighborhood that had somehow remained intact through decades of surrounding demolition and reconstruction. The houses were so close together a man could touch two by standing between and extending his arms, but the street was very dark and quiet. Bolan imagined entire families had probably grown up on this overlooked and forgotten strip. The house Gracho had entered was a Cape Cod design with full shed dormer in the back. Bolan was familiar with the standard floor plan consisting of four rooms downstairs and two or three bedrooms on the second floor. A center staircase immediately inside the front door would lead to the bedrooms.

Shades were drawn over every window, but lights were on in all the downstairs rooms. The flickering of bluish light squeezing out the edge of the shade in the front right room led Bolan to believe that someone was watching television.

With a glance to both sides to ensure there was no activity at the immediate neighbors' houses, Bolan moved as silently as a shadow to the rear of the house. As he expected, there was a bulkhead out back through which he could gain access into the cellar. The metal door was secured with a hasp and padlock, which Bolan studied in the almost complete darkness, concluding that the lock would not withstand the force of a 9 mm Parabellum round. It was a method he had used occasionally, but it wasn't something Bolan liked doing. The risks of an errant ricochet, or of the lock causing a loud sound when it shattered, made using his Beretta as a master key a dangerous choice.

He stepped back and surveyed the windows, searching in vain for a better entry. Gracho was armed, maybe the abbot also was, which meant when Bolan entered the living area, he'd be carrying the tranquilizer pistol in one hand and his Beretta in the other.

Bolan was confident in his ability to put the dart on a dime-sized target at more than a hundred feet. In two nylon loops sewn onto the outside of the pouch containing the pistol, he carried spare darts in the unlikely event he might need them, but reloading would require precious seconds at a time when he might be under fire. The best scenario would be if he obtained positive identification prior to shooting the first dart. Bolan recalled the image of Abbot Gabriel's face on the computer screen at Stony Man Farm, etching it into his brain. If all else failed, Bolan would wound to disable with the Beretta 93-R.

As he returned to the bulkhead, he was confident with the number of options he held.

Bolan placed the Beretta on the bulkhead's surface so he could jam the business end of the sound suppressor against the lock where it looped through the hasp. Pushing as hard as he could so there would be minimum jump when the round struck, he turned his head to the side and squeezed the trigger. The lock rattled and fell open, the 9 mm bullet slicing through the metal as cleanly as if he had used a bolt cutter. He removed the lock's remnants, which were hot from the round's energy, and opened the bulkhead enough to step through, closing it quietly behind.

Wooden stairs led from ground level into the pitch-black

basement. Drawing the dart gun from its pouch, Bolan descended, wiping cobwebs from his face as moved forward. Rough wooden stairs to the first floor stood in the center of the basement, leading either directly into the kitchen or to a hallway running behind the front rooms. On silent feet, Bolan ascended the stairs, a weapon in each hand.

At the top of the staircase, Bolan turned the doorknob and slowly pushed the door open, stepping into a small hallway behind the front rooms. Directly in front of him was a small bathroom, to his right a den. The kitchen was on his left. Lights were on in every room, and Gracho, who was sitting at the kitchen table, lunged for the pistol placed in its shoulder holster on the counter next to the sink.

Bolan's 93-R coughed once, the 9 mm round drilling a neat hole into the side of Gracho's face right below his cheekbone, sending him straight to the linoleum floor.

From the front room, someone called out.

"Brother Ernest? Are you all right?"

The absence of other voices led Bolan to believe the abbot was alone, and he dashed toward the front room where he thought someone was watching television. As he burst through the doorway, he made positive identification with the image he recalled from the computer screens.

Gabriel had on black pants and a white T-shirt. He was looking Bolan's way, standing at attention with the hint of an odd smile on his face as he forcefully clenched his jaw. Bolan raised his tranquilizer pistol and fired the dart a millisecond after the abbot began his collapse, hitting him in the neck as he went down to the carpeted floor.

A bitter almond odor reached Bolan's nostrils. He rushed forward, pried the abbot's mouth open, and tried sweeping the saliva laced with hydrocyanic acid off the abbot's tongue. After a few seconds, he realized it was too late. Gabriel had been prepared, with a capsule embedded in one of his teeth, waiting for a soldier of the Beast.

Bolan slapped the floor angrily, pulled his cell phone from his pocket and speed-dialed Brognola.

"He's dead," Bolan said. "Cyanide suicide capsule."

"I got the address from Akira. I'm sending a team in now to see if there's anything there that can lead us to the virus."

As Brognola spoke, Bolan could hear the sounds of vehicles arriving outside.

"Get back here, Striker. We found their house in Newport."

18

An hour and a half south of Boston, Interstate 24 left Massachusetts and crossed the Sakonnet Bridge onto Aquidneck Island, one of Narragansett Bay's jewels. With Newport on the far end and Portsmouth on the northern tip, the island drew visitors to Rhode Island from around the world to vacation in an environment where jazz, polo, luxury yachts, and mansions built during America's gilded age by the likes of Vanderbilt and Rockefeller, were part of the everyday ambiance.

Bolan drove past the Montaup Country Club with its sweeping vistas of the bay and the Mount Hope Bridge, and continued south through equestrian country and the Newport vineyards. He turned left onto Bellevue Avenue, passing the International Tennis Hall of Fame, housed in a section of what was once the Newport Casino. Along the entire length of Bellevue, from the extravagant mansions to the Hotel Viking, restored buildings with fancy facades crafted by Italian and French artisans a century earlier bespoke of a bygone era when America had a class of royalty that ruled industry.

Beyond the mansions, Bellevue turned into Ocean Drive, off of which the Newport Country Club was situated. The house Bolan was looking for was beyond the out of bounds marker for the thirteenth hole, a mile into the woods running parallel to the ocean.

He pulled into a state commons a few minutes after passing the country club's perimeter fences, drove to the far end of the parking lot and switched off the engine.

On the common, more than two dozen people were flying high-tech multitiered kites that soared and performed intricate maneuvers in the steady wind gusting off the water. Bolan watched them for a few moments, wondering when he had last laughed the way one of the men with two children was laughing as he helped the kids work the big plastic handles that controlled their kites' movements. A woman returned to them from the parking lot, carrying a food basket she had taken from the trunk of their car. She placed the basket on one of the picnic tables a short distance away and ran to join them.

The trunk of Bolan's Lincoln Towncar held the required hardware for him to accomplish the night's destruction. For now, he thought as he looked away from the happy family, all he needed was the pair of night-vision goggles resting on the seat beside him.

Barbara Price had been dead right in her assessment of how to find the Forty Martyrs. Following the mission controller's suggestion, Tokaido had hacked into the databases of the three major supermarkets servicing Aquidneck Island, merged and sorted their data, and found that all three were delivering foodstuffs to an eight thousand square foot mansion set on sixteen acres of oceanfront property. Thirteen acres surrounding the estate on its nonocean sides were woodlands, ensuring that the homestead was quite isolated from the rest of the world. Satellite photos taken during top secret flyovers directed by the President had all but confirmed the location where the late abbot's couriers of death were preparing themselves for a deployment intended to kill millions. Bolan's immediate mission was to provide on-the-ground absolute verification before he unleashed the firestorm.

As he stepped out of his car, he slid the goggles into his windbreaker's large front pocket. The only weapon he carried was his Beretta 93-R. For the reconnaissance mission he was about to begin, the 9 mm handgun with three spare 20-round clips of steel-jacketed Parabellum ammunition was sure to be adequate. With a quick glance around the moderately crowded parking lot, he walked to a path a few feet to the left of his car and entered the woods.

Once under the shade of the green canopy, he walked quickly and with purpose, anxious to finish not only this afternoon's mission, but the entire affair that had started at the vineyard in France. As he moved deeper into the woods, and the sounds of ocean surf faded behind him, he recalled the conversation he, Hal Brognola and Barbara Price had shared at Stony Man Farm.

Upon searching the house where Bolan had found Abbot Gabriel the previous night, Brognola's people discovered, among other things, a laptop with encrypted e-mail. It took Kurtzman's team no time to decode the messages. One indicated that the final component for the three-part virus had been received in Newport less than one hour before Bolan had entered the Fullerton Street residence. The message confirmed that the first deployment of three couriers to Los Angeles could take place within a week. Another e-mail confirmed the purchase of three one-way tickets on American Airlines from T. F. Green airport to LAX for the next day.

"They'll probably wait until the last minute in order to give themselves more time to get to their target cities before the virus breaks out, but we have no way of knowing they haven't already mixed the components together," Brognola said in the Farm's War Room. "Or if any members have infected themselves."

"I understand," Bolan answered.

"Will you need help?"

"No one should have to do this. I can get it done."

"I'll have backup standing by. You don't have to worry about outsiders."

"I can get it done," Bolan repeated.

"Will you be using special weapons?" Price asked.

He thought for a moment before answering. "I want an XM-8." He was referring to the U.S. Army's newest model to replace the M-16/M-4 family of rifles.

"Okay. Baseline carbine?" Price asked.

"Compact. I also want a full clip of orvilles for the Desert Eagle."

Price's response was a tight-lipped nod. Because of their inherent instability, she didn't like it when anyone on the Stony Man team used orvilles, but she wasn't about to question Bolan on his choice of weaponry.

Among covert groups operating outside the bounds of international laws and conventions, "orville" was the nickname for a highly explosive round that had been reamed out to make space for a glass ampule containing a wet paste of picric acid.

The theory behind an orville—which took the scientists in the CIA laboratories at Langley years to perfect even to its imperfect state—was that upon firing, the ampule shattered, allowing the bullet's heat to dry the acid into an extremely volatile yellow salt that reacted readily with the slug's lead. The chemical reaction produced an unstable explosive with more potential energy than TNT or nitroglycerin.

"While we're thinking along those lines, I'll also want two clips of Raufies for the XM-8."

Bolan thought for a moment, conjuring up an image of completion and how he could bring that future state to the present. Recalling the success he and LaFontaine had achieved in Australia, he said, "I'll use C-4 plastique to finish. Four quarter pounders, number-two blasting caps with RF microchip fuses, concurrent detonation."

All the hardware he requested was in the trunk of his vehicle, parked a short distance from the kite fliers, waiting for the opportunity to do what it had been created to do.

The four-story contemporary house was a conglomeration of chrome and glass intersecting to form asymmetrical angles and towers. The structure stood in a clearing facing the ocean, the wall on the water side made entirely of glass. When it came into view through the trees, Bolan dropped to one knee and studied the approach the way a golfer and caddy study the course before an important tournament.

There was a wide strip of beach on the ocean side, below a lip of lawn that would provide adequate cover if he low-crawled. The backyard was long, wide and open, affording unobstructed fields of fire. An attack would be more successful originating from the beach or the sides, where he wouldn't be exposed for as long a period of time after leaving the woods.

A detached four-car garage stood approximately fifty yards from the house. As Bolan watched, one of the Order's members exited the garage's side door and walked across the lawn to the house. Without using a key, he opened the front door and disappeared inside. There were no roving guards, a condition Bolan would have to make sure was the same when he returned at night. It was possible that the Order, as inexperienced in the nuts and bolts of combat as they were, believed they had reached a point where they were unstoppable. Or perhaps they thought God was their sentry. Whatever the reason, Bolan hoped there would be no guards that night.

The Executioner reached into his windbreaker's front pocket for the night-vision goggles. Once they were in place, he switched them into IR mode, and scanned the scene before him. The building was protected on all sides except the ocean with IR grids similar to the ones that had foiled his attempt to probe the Order's facility in Boston.

He noted the location and width of the security nets, and was somewhat surprised that the garage was completely unprotected.

In his mind, Bolan rehearsed the upcoming battle. He would surely catch them by surprise. If the initial attack played out well, he would drive them into the backyard or force them to attempt an escape by car. Those who remained inside would die when the plastique reduced the house to a smoldering tangle of chrome and broken glass.

Removing the goggles, he inched away until the trees obstructed his view and he felt safe rising to his full height for the walk back to the common. Brognola had rented him a room at a hotel in downtown Newport. Checking his watch, the warrior saw there was time for him to get a few hours of sleep before going to work.

Later, he would shatter an insane cult's twisted dreams and save kite fliers throughout America from a horrible fate.

AT A FEW MINUTES after midnight, the woods were so dark Bolan couldn't see his hand in front of his face. A cold wind, smelling of the sea, was blowing inland from a distant ocean storm. The combat veteran was dressed entirely in black, his face smeared with camouflage paint. He was in full battle dress, the pouches on his web belt containing everything he needed for a scorched earth blitz. On his right hip, he carried his Desert Eagle, loaded with .44-caliber death. A magazine of orvilles was stored in a watertight plastic wrap inside his left ammo pouch. The intent was to keep them moist until they were needed.

The reason Price didn't like the volatile rounds was because a weapon's ammo port sometimes became hot enough to crack an interior ampule while the bullet was still in its magazine. When that happened, the water in the picric paste evaporated, the remaining chemical reacted with the lead, and the resulting explosion not only killed the person holding the weapon, but everyone else within twenty feet. Bolan planned to use the orvilles to initiate his attack, firing the entire magazine. After that, he'd rely on the forty Raufies he carried for the XM-8 to provide extra fireworks.

Modeled after the Nordic Ammunition Company's Raufoss .50-caliber multipurpose round, the 5.56 mm copper-jacketed bullets possessed on a smaller scale the same incendiary and armor-piercing capabilities as their larger prototype. With a tungsten carbide hard core and a pyrotechnically initiated fuse that delayed detonation of the inner charge until after initial target penetration, the rounds were not as powerful as Bolan's orvilles, but when they hit a specific target such as the gas tank of a car, they were as effective as a stick of dynamite.

In his shoulder holster, Bolan carried the Beretta 93-R

and slung across his back was the XM-8. Bolan had pulled on his night-vision goggles while standing on the thirteenth green at Newport, where he entered the woods after leaving his car hidden behind a stand of pines lining the course. The technology amplified even the tiniest amount of ambient light into a bright landscape, and the Executioner had no problem seeing into the distance as he threaded his way through the trees.

The first thing he noticed coming upon the house was the light spilling out from under one of the garage doors. His plan was to open the assault from the beach with the orvilles intended to set the inside of the house on fire, but first he would have to take care of anyone, including guards, who were up and about the grounds. He hadn't brought a sound suppressor, knowing that the noise of the wind blowing nonstop through the woods would be sufficient to muffle the sounds of 9 mm rounds.

Staying close to the trees, he sneaked close to the garage. There was a window on the back side against the woods, affording him the opportunity to creep forward from his concealment directly into the shadow of the garage. Pressed tight against the back wall, he inched his eye to the bottom right corner of the windowpane and peered within.

Directly in front of him in the first bay was the Porsche Cayenne. The far bay also housed an SUV, an oversized white Cadillac that gleamed under the overhead lights. Three men were standing in the two parking spaces between the cars, smoking cigarettes and talking. They were all armed with FN Five-seveN pistols carried in shoulder holsters.

Bolan ducked as soon as he registered the scene. Drawing the Beretta from its holster, he walked quickly to the door, pulled it open and calmly entered. He was two steps inside before the men realized he was not one of their own, and one began to shout while they all grabbed frantically for their pistols. The one who had started to say something was rudely interrupted when a 9 mm slug slammed into his forehead, abruptly ending the thought. He toppled over, eyes wide and unseeing.

Short-lived terror registered on the faces of the other two, who never did get their weapons out of their holsters, as Bolan squeezed the Beretta's trigger twice in rapid order, hitting the first man directly in the heart. The force of the slug striking midbody threw him three feet toward the shiny Cadillac, where he landed dead with his hand on the butt of his weapon. The third shot from Bolan's Beretta pierced the carotid artery of the final man, loosing a crimson flood. His body whipped around in response to the slug's punch as he fell, his rotary motion shotgunning the side of the white SUV with a fan-shaped pattern of tiny red dots.

Bolan turned on his heel and left the garage, turning off the lights on his way out. The battle had commenced.

The sand on the narrow beach was hard and wet, making it easy for Bolan to crawl to a position dead center to the house. Lights were on in a few rooms, causing the tower to stand out against the blackness beyond, and although it was past midnight, more than a dozen intended couriers of death were still up. Some were reading; a few were sitting in small groups talking and some were watching televisions, which appeared to be installed in every room. FN P-90 submachine guns were stacked against the wall in various rooms, and most men were armed with the same model pistols as the three in the garage wore.

Bolan pulled his Desert Eagle from his hip, ejected the magazine and swapped it for the one loaded with orvilles.

Taking a deep breath to steady himself before all hell broke loose, he opened fire, moving from left to right, bottom to top, splitting the night's calm with eardrum-pulsing explosions that spewed fire and smoke throughout the building's interior. Howls of pain mixed with shrieks of fury poured from the house following his opening salvo, and Bolan found himself immediately under fire from all four floors. While hugging the sand, he ejected the spent clip and rammed a fresh one home before crawling back to the woods as fast as he could, staying low under the narrow cover of the lawn's protective berm.

Men armed with P-90 submachine guns came running from the house, firing their weapons wildly in all directions. Bolan brought the XM-8 into his shoulder and engaged targets of opportunity, weaving the weapon's automatic stutter around single shots as merited. The XM-8's muzzle-blasts revealed his position, and he came under attack as half a dozen gunmen hosed the area around him with a steady spray of 5.7 mm lead.

Bolan remained low, waiting for an opportune time to dash to a better position. When his combat senses told him there was a split-second lull, he burst forward, emptying the assault rifle's magazine in a thundering drumroll as he launched himself to a spot equidistant from the house and garage.

At his new position, he was able to see two groups of three each attempting a flanking move around the garage. They had apparently run straight to the distant woods, and were about to try an open field dash across the yard to get behind him. Flames from the burning house were licking the night clouds, lighting the entire clearing with flickering orange light. The stink of cordite and death accosted Bolan's nostrils as he waited patiently, allowing the gunmen to progress into the open. When they made their ill-fated move, he cut them down like wheat in a field, keeping the trigger of the XM-8 depressed until the bolt clicked open on an empty chamber. In one fluid move, he released the empty magazine with his right thumb while shoving a fresh 20-rounder into the weapon's ammo port with his left hand.

Seven or eight defenders had taken positions against the house, and Bolan directed his fire toward them, emptying two clips at a rate of seven hundred rounds per minute. Hot brass poured from the XM-8's ejector port in a golden cascade, bouncing and spinning wildly on the pine-needle-coated ground as Bolan caressed his weapon's trigger. The 5.56 mm slugs found their targets, tumbling inside the victim's body upon impact and killing the enemy where they stood. By the time the last bullet in the XM-8's clip was fired, and the rifle's bolt finally clicked on air, the night held the acrid tang of combat. Through his night-vision goggles, Bolan could see corpses littering the property on three sides of the house.

A break in the gunfire came abruptly, and the only sound was the crackling of the flames racing through the expansive house. Bolan decided the time had arrived for the C-4 plastique, and made a serpentine charge for the building's near corner. When he was twenty feet away, he was engaged by a gunman firing from the back lawn, and he threw himself into a dive, answering the attack with an effective burst from the Desert Eagle.

When the man on the lawn fell silent, Bolan scrambled forward, smashed a wad of C-4 onto the edge of the house's corner, and jabbed a blasting cap into the glob.

Bolan drew his Beretta and ran in a crouch past the

house's shattered glass front. Inside, he could see dozens of bodies as he raced toward the far side. Halfway there, a dozen men trapped inside the inferno began firing at him as he ran, forcing him to dive for the sand as bullets snapped the air above his head. He hit the beach sand hard, rolling on impact to the cover of the short overhang from the lawn, both his handguns spitting death in response.

One of his victims on the third floor toppled from the opening where a floor-to-ceiling pane of glass had been, his corpse bouncing once upon hitting the manicured grass forty feet below before coming to rest. Bolan continued firing as fast as he could pull the triggers. Bullets ricocheted into the night, turning the usually serene ocean setting into a hell-fire zone.

His hands a blur as he replaced one magazine after another, Bolan continued to make progress toward the far corner of the house, where he was able to plant the second C-4 charge. The enemy was near defeat by the time Bolan moved to the back corner, where he came under fire from two gunmen hiding behind trees. He turned on their positions, blazing away with the Desert Eagle and Beretta, sending well-aimed rounds that caught them as they peeked out from behind their cover.

The battlefield fell silent again as Bolan planted the third wad of C-4, and he began to wonder if he had killed them all. His answer came with the roar of automobile engines. Quickly holstering his pistols, he pulled the XM-8 into his shoulder while reaching into his pouch for a clip loaded with Raufoss rounds. The SUVs came crashing through the garage doors together, tires smoking and screaming as they lay thick strips of rubber onto the driveway's surface. Bolan waited for them to separate, then engaged each with a burst of incendiary armor-piercing rounds. The Porsche Cayenne exploded into a fireball that flew two feet into the air before overturning and crashing in a flaming tangle of steel. The Cadillac's fate was no better, as the rounds found the fuel tank, exploding with a thunderous force that shook shards of glass from the house's burning frame. Bolan sprinted to the remaining corner, planted his final charge and ran toward the garage.

Once he reached the far side, he dived into a prone position behind the building, drew his Desert Eagle with his right hand, and fished the electronic detonator from one of the pouches on his web belt with his left. When he triggered the charges, the result was as stunning as it had been in Australia.

An enormous column of fire shot skyward as a shock wave rippled forth in all directions, snapping branches in the woods as if giants were walking the earth. The garage walls shook to the point where Bolan thought the structure might fall. When the force passed, he looked around the corner, searching for movement. The only sound was the twisting and shrieking of metal as the structure that had once been a glamorous house on the ocean folded in on itself, compressing to a smoking heap belching a steady stream of black smoke.

Brognola had told him that fire would kill the virus, but a team in HAZ MAT suits would soon be on-site to make sure there were no lethal remains while they counted the casualties.

Bolan remained in position for a good fifteen minutes, watching for survivors. When he was almost sure there were none, he got up and quickly walked the clearing's perimeter, his handguns drawn and ready for action. Upon completion of the border sweep, he holstered the weapons, confident that he had exterminated the Order of Raphael from the face of the Earth.

The Executioner stepped into the woods to begin his walk back to civilization as peace settled over the killing fields.

19

Dr. Robert Cafard lived with his wife and two teenage daughters on a small country estate twenty-three kilometers outside Paris. The library, where he worked for a few hours every night after his wife and children went to bed, was a cherry-paneled room in a far wing of the house filled from floor-to-ceiling with bookcases. It was a warm cozy space conducive to deep thought that smelled of leather, polished wood, and other things old and rich. Against the far window, through which the Executioner had entered after circumventing the estate's alarm system using an electronic device Kurtzman had given him, an antique desk sat in front of a burgundy leather executive chair.

Crouched behind a love seat upholstered in a flowery blue print, Bolan held his silenced Beretta 93-R in his left hand, and in his right, a tranquilizer pistol. He was dressed entirely in black, wearing a long sleeved cotton T-shirt with a fully loaded hypodermic needle ready for use in the breast pocket.

As Bolan awaited Cafard, he sincerely hoped the doctor would remain true to habit by coming alone. One of Brognola's men had been watching the library for more than a week, and during that time Cafard had always come by himself.

Outside the door, Bolan heard footsteps approaching. It was a single set coming quickly down the tiled hallway, the timing between steps telling Bolan it was someone approximately Cafard's height. The library door opened, then closed softly as if the doctor was afraid he might awaken his family with too much noise from this distant wing.

When his target was three feet inside the library, Bolan stood to full height, extended the pistol an arm's length to the front and pulled the trigger. Cafard's eyes widened in surprise at the presence of an intruder in his house, but before he could utter a single word, he fell to the floor like a sack of grain.

Bolan moved quickly. After locking the library door, he returned to his unconscious victim. Using a fireman's carry, he hefted the doctor onto his shoulders and transported him across the room to the leather executive chair. The armrests were at a perfect height for Bolan's intentions. He placed his Beretta on the desk and went to work.

From his pocket, he withdrew nylon tie wraps of various lengths and used them to quickly secure Cafard to the chair. With tie wraps around his chest, neck, forearms, thighs and shins, he was completely immobile except for his fingers. When the soldier was satisfied with the ties, he inserted a cloth gag into Cafard's mouth, tying it securely behind his head.

Glancing at his watch, he removed the hypodermic needle from his shirt pocket while pulling his cell phone from a holder on his belt.

"Yes," Brognola said, answering Bolan's speed dial. The man from the Justice Department was approximately six miles away, standing in a bank vault with Dr. Richard Hannigan, the former deputy to Terrance MacPherson on the

Australian mouse pox project. The walls of the bank vault were lined from floor-to-ceiling with safe-deposit boxes, each with four tumblers set into the front door of the box directly below a brass plate engraved with a three-digit number. In the middle of the vault, a rolling ladder was available to reach those in the higher rows.

They had brought with them a sample of the substance MacPherson had produced for the Order of Raphael in Sydney, and a test kit that both Hannigan and Sonia Zagorski guaranteed would determine within seconds the presence of an effective antidote. By itself, MacPherson's compound presented no danger to the men, but ever the scientist, Hannigan was insisting on proper lab procedure. He was wearing latex gloves, and every piece of his test kit had been sterilized.

Bolan removed the plastic shield from the hypodermic's tip, plunged the needle into Cafard's arm and depressed the plunger. After withdrawing the needle, he replaced its shield over the tip, wrapped the entire unit into a handkerchief and shoved it into his pants pocket.

The wait was not long. Cafard stirred, appeared to press against his restraints, then abruptly opened his eyes. His breathing immediately became quick and panicked, and he began making noises through his nose.

"Calm down," Bolan said in a quiet voice by his ear. "I'm not going to kill you, and I won't harm your wife and daughters if you are quiet."

At the mention of his family, Cafard froze. A single tear escaped from his left eye and rolled down his cheek where it hung for a second before falling onto his chest. He took a few deep breaths, which appeared to settle him, but a sweat broke out on his brow, and the vein in his temple throbbed.

"Very good," Bolan said softly. "Now listen carefully. I have people standing in the vault of the National Bank, waiting for you to tell us the combination to a safe-deposit box we believe contains the antidote."

Cafard attempted to shake his head against the restraining ties.

"If we are correct in our belief, you and your family will live. The United States will possess the antidote, and all will be well. If you say it is not there, I will bring your wife into this room and tie her up exactly as you are. Then I will bring in your two lovely daughters, and very slowly, in front of you and your wife, I will kill each of them in an extremely painful way. I will make their suffering last all night before I also kill you and your wife."

Cafard sucked in a great breath of air, and his eyes grew wild. His gaze darted swiftly around the room as if he believed the key to his deliverance might be among the volumes lining the walls.

"If you understand what I am saying, raise your right index finger. That is how you'll say yes."

Cafard's finger raised off the armrest.

"Good. Lower your finger."

The man did as he was told.

"For the sake of your family, I hope the antidote is in that vault. Is it there?"

Cafard's finger signaled that it was.

"Listen carefully. One of the men in the vault is a scientist who has a test that will tell us if you've directed us to the true antidote or to a box containing a decoy. If his test works, you and your family will live. If the test does not work, it will be very, very bad for your daughters."

Cafard was trembling, and sweat was running in rivulets

down his face. He squeezed his eyes shut in response to the salty moisture and took a deep, ragged breath. He appeared to gag for an instant, and his breath hitched in his throat, but Bolan waited patiently. Cafard settled back down again. When the doctor's breathing became steady, Bolan continued.

"I will start counting, beginning with zero. When I reach the first number of the box you want us to open, raise your finger. Think now of the number on that box. If you make a mistake, you and your family will die. Think."

Bolan paused for a long second before starting to count in a soft, calm voice.

When Bolan had repeated the process four times, he picked up his cell phone from the desktop and said, "Four, one, eight, six."

Brognola repeated the numbers, and Bolan placed the phone back out of the way.

"Now we need the numbers for the four tumblers," he said. "If the combination opens the box, your family lives. If not, they die a long horrible death."

The doctor swallowed hard, his Adam's apple scraping against the nylon tie.

Bolan repeated the process they had used to find the box.

"Seven, five, seven, zero," he said into the cell phone.

Brognola repeated the combination. Keeping the cell phone to his ear, Bolan sat on the edge of the desk where Cafard could see him.

"Now we wait. I hope our scientist is as smart as the ones you and your brother forced to create a disease that you intended to use against millions of innocent men, women and children. Thousands of girls just like your daughters would have died. Think of that, Doctor. You tried to murder millions of people."

Bolan raised his eyebrows and said into the phone, "Are you sure? Is there documentation? Is Hannigan absolutely sure?"

He glanced at Cafard, who visibly relaxed, sensing that the test had proved the antidote was genuine.

"Good. Come take this guy away."

Bolan snapped his cell phone closed, picked up his Beretta and said, "You told us the truth." He started walking away, then paused and said, "You are about to disappear. Your family will never know what happened to you."

It took Cafard a few seconds to understand what Bolan had said.

Bolan calmly moved beyond the desk, grabbed the thin cord attached to a grappling hook embedded in the window's frame, and swung himself to the outside, snatching the electronic unit off the wall as he passed. While he lowered himself to the ground, he pondered the danger inherent in a world of ever-advancing technology. Without question, science held the promise to improve the lives of countless people around the world, but it also possessed a dark side, capable of forever shifting the global balance of power. New knowledge and techniques that could have enabled a team of scientists to address a specific rodent problem had been corrupted by a terrorist cult to produce a product that threatened humankind's very existence.

Bolan knew that technology in all fields would continue to advance, presenting unforeseen opportunities for both good and evil. When he reached the ground and turned to walk away, the Executioner was equally certain that for as long as he breathed, he would be available to wage battle against the forces threatening the free world.

TAKE 'EM FREE

2 action-packed novels plus a mystery bonus

NO RISK

NO OBLIGATION TO BUY